The Last of the Mohicans

最後的摩根戰士

商務印書館

Name of Book: The Last of the Mohicans
Author: James Fenimore Cooper
Text adaptation, notes and activities: Gina D.B. Clemen
Editors: Claudia Fiocco, Rebecca Raynes
Design and art direction: Nadia Maestri
Computer graphics: Simona Corniola
Illustrations: Alfredo Belli
Edition: ©2003 Black Cat Publishing
          an imprint of Cideb Editrice, Genoa, Canterbury

系 列 名：Black Cat 優質英語階梯閱讀 · Level 5
書　　名：最後的摩根戰士
顧　　問：Angeli Lau
責任編輯：傅　伊
封面設計：張　毅　曹　磊
出　　版：商務印書館（香港）有限公司
　　　　　香港筲箕灣耀興道3號東滙廣場8樓
　　　　　http://www.commercialpress.com.hk
印　　刷：中華商務彩色印刷有限公司
　　　　　香港新界大埔汀麗路36號中華商務印刷大廈
版　　次：2003 年 8 月第 1 版第 1 次印刷
　　　　　© 2003 商務印書館（香港）有限公司
　　　　　ISBN 962 07 1663 9
　　　　　Printed in Hong Kong

版權所有　不得翻印

出版説明

　　本館一向倡導優質閱讀，近年來連續推出了以"Q"為標識的 "Quality English Learning 優質英語學習"系列，其中《讀名著學英語》叢書，更是香港書展入選好書，讀者反響令人鼓舞。推動社會閱讀風氣，推動英語經典閱讀，藉閱讀拓廣世界視野，提高英語水平，已經成為一種潮流。

　　然良好閱讀習慣的養成非一日之功，大多數初、中級程度的讀者，常視直接閱讀厚重的原著為畏途。如何給年輕的讀者提供切實的指引和幫助，如何既提供優質的學習素材，又提供名師的教學方法，是當下社會關注的重要問題。針對這種情況，本館特別延請香港名校名師，根據多年豐富的教學經驗，精選海外適合初、中級英語程度讀者的優質經典讀物，有系統地出版了這套叢書，名為《Black Cat 優質英語階梯閱讀》。

　　《Black Cat 優質英語階梯閱讀》體現了香港名校名師堅持經典學習的教學理念，以及多年行之有效的學習方法。既有經過改寫和縮寫的經典名著，又有富創意的現代作品；既有精心設計的聽、說、讀、寫綜合練習，又有豐富的歷史文化知識；既有彩色插圖、繪圖和照片，又有英美專業演員朗讀作品的 CD。適合口味不同的讀者享受閱讀之樂，欣賞經典之美。

　　《Black Cat 優質英語階梯閱讀》由淺入深，逐階提升，好像參與一個尋寶遊戲，入門並不難，但要真正尋得寶藏，需要投入，更需要堅持。只有置身其中的人，才能體味純正英語的魅力，領略得到真寶的快樂。當英語閱讀成為自己生活的一部分，英語水平的提高自然水到渠成。

商務印書館 (香港) 有限公司
編輯部

使用説明

① 應該怎樣選書？

按閱讀興趣選書

《Black Cat 優質英語階梯閱讀》精選世界經典作品，也包括富於創意的現代作品；既有膾炙人口的小説、戲劇，又有非小説類的文化知識讀物，品種豐富，內容多樣，適合口味不同的讀者挑選自己感興趣的書，享受閱讀的樂趣。

按英語程度選書

《Black Cat 優質英語階梯閱讀》現設 Level 1 至 Level 6，由淺入深，涵蓋初、中級英語程度。讀物分級採用了國際上通用的劃分標準，主要以詞彙（vocabulary）和結構（structures）劃分。

Level 1 至 Level 3 出現的詞彙較淺顯，相對深的核心詞彙均配上中文解釋，節省讀者查找詞典的時間，以專心理解正文內容。在註釋的幫助下，讀者若能流暢地閱讀正文內容，就不用擔心這一本書程度過深。

Level 1 至 Level 3 出現的動詞時態形式和句子結構比較簡單。動詞時態形式以現在時（present simple）、現在時進行式（present continuous）、過去時（past simple）為主，句子結構大部分是簡單句（simple sentences）。此外，還包括比較級和最高級（comparative and superlative forms）、可數和不可數名詞（countable and uncountable nouns）以及冠詞（articles）等語法知識點。

Level 4 至 Level 6 出現的動詞時態形式，以現在完成時（present perfect）、現在完成時進行式（present perfect continuous）、過去完成時（past perfect continuous）為主，句子結構大部分是複合句（compound sentences）、條件從句（1st and 2nd conditional sentences）等。此外，還包括情態動詞（modal verbs）、被動形式（passive forms）、動名詞（gerunds）、

短語動詞（phrasal verbs）等語法知識點。

　　根據上述的語法範圍，讀者可按自己實際的英語水平，如詞彙量、語法知識、理解能力、閱讀能力等自主選擇，不再受制於學校年級劃分或學歷高低的約束，完全根據個人需要選擇合適的讀物。

② 怎樣提高閱讀效果？

　　閱讀的方法主要有兩種：一是泛讀，二是精讀。兩者各有功能，適當地結合使用，相輔相成，有事半功倍之效。

　　泛讀，指閱讀大量適合自己程度（可稍淺，但不能過深）、不同內容、風格、體裁的讀物，但求明白內容大意，不用花費太多時間鑽研細節，主要作用是多接觸英語，減輕對它的生疏感，鞏固以前所學過的英語，讓腦子在潛意識中吸收詞彙用法、語法結構等。

　　精讀，指小心認真地閱讀內容精彩、組織有條理、遣詞造句又正確的作品，着重點在於理解 "準確" 及 "深入"，欣賞其精彩獨到之處。精讀時，可充分利用書中精心設計的練習，學習掌握有用的英語詞彙和語法知識。精讀後，可再花十分鐘朗讀其中一小段有趣的文字，邊唸邊細心領會文字的結構和意思。

　　《Black Cat 優質英語階梯閱讀》中的作品均值得精讀，如時間有限，不妨嘗試每兩個星期泛讀一本，輔以每星期挑選書中一章精彩的文字精讀。要學好英語，持之以恆地泛讀和精讀英文是最有效的方法。

③ 本系列的練習與測試有何功能？

　　《Black Cat 優質英語階梯閱讀》特別注重練習的設計，為讀者考慮周到，切合實用需求，學習功能強。每章後均配有訓練聽、説、讀、寫四項技能的練習，分量、難度恰到好處。

聽力練習分兩類，一是重聽故事回答問題，二是聆聽主角對話、書信朗讀、或模擬記者訪問後寫出答案，旨在以生活化的練習形式逐步提高聽力。每本書均配有 CD 提供作品朗讀，朗讀者都是專業演員，英國作品由英國演員錄音，美國作品由美國演員錄音，務求增加聆聽的真實感和感染力。多聆聽英式和美式英語兩種發音，可讓讀者熟悉二者的差異，逐漸培養分辨英美發音的能力，提高聆聽理解的準確度。此外，模仿錄音朗讀故事或模仿主人翁在戲劇中的對白，都是訓練口語能力的好方法。

閱讀理解練習形式多樣化，有縱橫字謎、配對、填空、字句重組等等，注重訓練讀者的理解、推敲和聯想等多種閱讀技能。

寫作練習尤具新意，教讀者使用網式圖示（spidergrams）記錄重點，採用問答、書信、電報、記者採訪等多樣化形式，鼓勵讀者動手寫作。

書後更設有升級測試（Exit Test）及答案，供讀者檢查學習效果。充分利用書中的練習和測試，可全面提升聽、說、讀、寫四項技能。

④ 本系列還能提供甚麼幫助？

《Black Cat 優質英語階梯閱讀》提倡豐富多元的現代閱讀，巧用書中提供的資訊，有助於提升英語理解力，擴闊視野。

每本書都設有專章介紹相關的歷史文化知識，經典名著更有作者生平、社會背景等資訊。書內富有表現力的彩色插圖、繪圖和照片，使閱讀充滿趣味，部分加上如何解讀古典名畫的指導，增長見識。有的書還提供一些與主題相關的網址，比如關於不同國家的節慶源流的網址，讓讀者多利用網上資源增進知識。

Contents

   First Certificate in English Examination-style exercises

T: GRADES 6-7   Trinity-style exercises (Grades 6-7)

This story is recorded in full. 故事錄音

 This symbol indicates the chapters and exercises featured on the accompanying CD. 文章和聽力練習的錄音標記

 These symbols indicate the beginning and end of the extracts linked to the listening activities. 聽力練習開始和結束的標記

*James Fenimore Coope*r by John Wesley Jarvis.

A Note on
James Fenimore Cooper

James Fenimore Cooper was born in Burlington, New Jersey, on September 15th, 1789. When he was only one year old, his family moved from Burlington to an enormous estate [1] on Otsego Lake, New York.

Although the boy lived in a beautiful house on a huge estate, his home was surrounded [2] by dense [3] forests and wilderness. As a boy, he learned to use the bow and arrow, [4] ride horseback, fish and shoot.

---

1. **estate** : large piece of land in the country.
2. **surrounded** : encircled.
3. **dense** : crowded together in great numbers.
4. **bow and arrow** :

Members of the Oneida Indian tribe still lived in the forest near his home. He met several Indians during his youth. His boyhood experiences formed the background for many of his novels.

In 1801 he attended a Yale preparatory school for two years. Then he spent three years in the United States Navy.

In 1811 Cooper married Susan DeLancey. He was wealthy and lived as a gentleman farmer in the state of New York.

One evening he made a bet with his wife. He bet that he could write a book that was better than the boring book he was reading! In 1820 he wrote his first novel, *Precaution*, which was not an important work.

His second novel, *The Spy* (1821), was the first important historical novel about the American Revolution. In 1823 he published *The Pioneers*, the first of five books about the courageous frontier scout, [1] Natty Bumppo. These books were known as *The Leatherstocking Tales*. Natty Bumppo became a very popular character in Cooper's novels.

Cooper's best-known work, *The Last of the Mohicans*, was published in 1826. This great novel was based on an American folk-tale. [2] Here the character Natty Bumppo is called Hawkeye. With this novel, Cooper became world famous. *The Last of the Mohicans* had a great international appeal [3] because of its setting, its unforgettable characters, and its exciting plot. [4]

---

1. **frontier scout** : person who explored the unknown territory and located the position of the Indians.
2. **folk-tale** : popular story passed on by speech.
3. **appeal** : attraction or interest.
4. **plot** : connected events of a story.

Cooper and his wife sailed for Europe in 1826. In Paris he wrote *The Prairie* (1827), and *Notions of the Americans* (1828).

Upon his return to the United States, he wrote two more *Leatherstocking Tales*: *The Pathfinder* (1840), and *The Deerslayer* (1841).

Cooper died on September 16th, 1851, a day after his sixty-second birthday. He was America's first internationally famous novelist. He introduced readers everywhere to the reality and the excitement of the American frontier.

The courageous frontier scout became
a very popular figure in Cooper's novel.

Cooper and
the American Frontier

The American frontier and the people who settled in it form the background for Cooper's novels. His character studies of the Indians and the white men have always been appreciated by his readers.

A close friendship between a white man and an Indian is one of the most important themes in Cooper's books. Cooper presents the Indians as strong, courageous and honest. If they behave in any other way, then white men have corrupted them.

The Leatherstocking Tales is a series of five novels, that present the white hunter and frontier scout, Natty Bumppo. Natty is called many names in Cooper's books: Leatherstocking, Hawkeye, Deerslayer and Pathfinder. His character is that of the honest, loyal man of the frontier. He prefers the simple, natural rules of the Indians, to the complex and often cunning [1] ones of the white men.

Bumppo, who is a man of the forest, cannot live in a "civilized" environment. Therefore, he keeps moving west in the novels. He is always one step ahead of the civilization that follows him.

Natty's closest friends are the Indians, and particularly Chingachgook, the Mohican chief. [2] Natty and Chingachgook have incredible adventures together.

---

1. **cunning** : clever at deceiving people.
2. **Mohican chief** : Mohican leader of the tribe.

BLACK CAT ENGLISH CLUB

The Commercial Press (Hong Kong) Ltd.
9/F, Eastern Central Plaza,
3 Yiu Hing Road, Shau Kei Wan,
Hong Kong

BLACK CAT ENGLISH CLUB

Membership Application Form

BLACK CAT ENGLISH CLUB is for those who love English reading and seek for better English to share and learn with fun together.

Benefits offered:
- *Member Card*
- *Member badge, poster, bookmark*
- *Book discount coupon*
- *Black Cat English Reward Scheme*
- *English learning e-forum*
- *Surprise gift and more...*

Simply fill out the application form below and fax it back to 2565 1113.

Join Now! It's FREE exclusively for readers who have purchased *Black Cat English Readers* !

The book(or book set) that you have purchased: _____

English Name: _____ (Surname) _____ (Given Name)

Chinese Name: _____

Address: _____

Tel: _____ Fax: _____

Email: _____

Sex: ❏ Male   ❏ Female   (Login password for e-forum will be sent to this email address.)

Education Background: ❏ Primary 1-3   ❏ Primary 4-6   ❏ Junior Secondary Education (F1-3)
                     ❏ Senior Secondary Education (F4-5)   ❏ Matriculation
                     ❏ College   ❏ University or above

Age: ❏ 6 - 9   ❏ 10 - 12   ❏ 13 - 15   ❏ 16 - 18   ❏ 19 - 24   ❏ 25 - 34
     ❏ 35 - 44   ❏ 45 - 54   ❏ 55 or above

Occupation: ❏ Student   ❏ Teacher   ❏ White Collar   ❏ Blue Collar
             ❏ Professional   ❏ Manager   ❏ Business Owner   ❏ Housewife
             ❏ Others (please specify: _____)

As a member, what would you like **BLACK CAT ENGLISH CLUB** to offer:

❏ Member gathering/ party   ❏ English class with native teacher   ❏ English competition
❏ Newsletter   ❏ Online sharing   ❏ Book fair
❏ Book discount   ❏ Others (please specify: _____)

Other suggestions to **BLACK CAT ENGLISH CLUB**:

_____

Please sign here: _____

(Date: _____)

This deep friendship between a white man and an Indian was something completely new in Cooper's day. Indians were often seen as savages and enemies. Their culture, traditions and beliefs were almost unknown to the Americans of the 1800s. Cooper was able to present the Indians in another light.

Cooper knew that the world of the American Indians was destined to disappear. The westward movement of American civilization could not be stopped. Cooper's feelings about American expansion were mixed. He was very worried about the destruction of the natural environment that comes with new settlements.

The signing of a treaty which shows the friendship between the white men and the Indians.

New settlements also meant less land for the American Indians, and more problems for them. But Cooper also believed that the immense American continent had to be settled, from east to west. He felt that the destiny of America was one of expansion and development.

1 Do you agree with Cooper about the destiny of America? Why/why not?

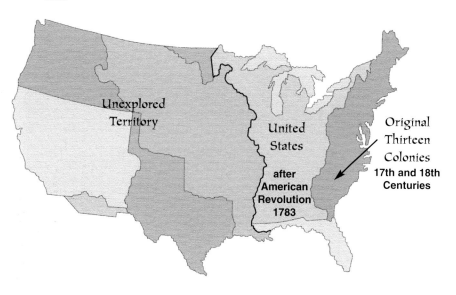

In FCE (Reading), Part 4 you will be asked which person is referred to in the extract.

Look back at Cooper and the American Frontier and match the definitions / sentences (1-8) to the correct person or people (A-F). There is an example at the beginning (0).

A = Americans

B = Cooper

C = Leatherstocking

D = Chingachgook

E = Deerslayer

F = Natty Bumppo

0. ☐B☐ Many readers have appreciated his character studies of the Indians and the white men.

1. ☐ He was a white hunter and frontier scout.

2. ☐ He was Natty's close friend.

3. ☐ He wrote *The Leatherstocking Tales*.

4. ☐ This was another name for Leatherstocking and Natty Bumppo.

5. ☐ They did not know about the Indian traditions and culture.

6. ☐ He believed that the immense American continent had to be settled.

7. ☐ He could not live in a "civilized" environment.

8. ☐ He was a Mohican chief.

1.
The Expedition[1]

Perhaps no other part of the North American wilderness was so difficult to conquer as the area along the Hudson River to the Canadian border. Thick, green forests, with every kind of tree, animal and bird covered the entire region. Numerous lakes and hundreds of rivers and streams formed a labyrinth. [2] Tall waterfalls, high cliffs and hidden caves completed the natural landscape. [3] Snowy winters and hot, humid summers were the typical climate.

1. **expedition** : a long journey for a special purpose.
2. **labyrinth** : a complicated set of paths and passages, through which it is difficult to find your way.
3. **landscape** : outdoor scenery.

1. The Expedition

It was difficult for the early colonists to settle in this area. It was even more difficult for soldiers to fight a war here. Only the Indians of the different tribes moved quickly and safely in this region.

It had been their home for centuries.

In 1754 the French and Indian War began in this region. In July 1757 Fort Henry was a small Anglo-American fort under the command of General Munro. General Munro's Indian scouts had reported to him that the enemy, the French and the Huron Indians, was numerous. Therefore he asked General Webb, commander of the larger Fort Edward, to send him more soldiers.

General Webb immediately sent a group of soldiers to General Munro. General Webb then asked young Major Heyward to accompany General Munro's two daughters to see their father. Cora Munro, a beautiful young woman with dark hair and dark eyes, was the oldest. Alice Munro, a delicate adolescent [1] with fair hair and blue eyes, was the youngest.

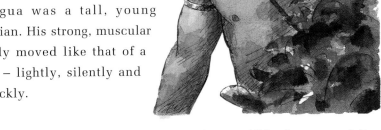

Major Heyward's Indian guide, Magua, led the expedition through the forest. Magua was a tall, young Indian. His strong, muscular body moved like that of a cat – lightly, silently and quickly.

1. **adolescent** : a young person who is no longer a child and not yet an adult.

The Last of the Mohicans

Magua walked ahead, following a secret path, while the others followed close behind. Alice and Cora rode two Narraganset horses. These horses were the most secure for riding in rough country and in forests. Magua moved with ease through the dense vegetation. [1]

Shortly after leaving Fort Edward, the group met a young white man who was also going to Fort Henry. He was a preacher [2] and a singing teacher of religious hymns. [3] He carried a prayer book and a pipe [4] with him. His name was David Gamut.

As they crossed the forest, Alice Munro said to Major Heyward, "I don't trust the eyes of the Indian guide Magua."

Major Heyward replied, "Magua is a friend. He is the only one who knows the secret way through this dangerous forest."

"I still don't like his eyes," Alice insisted.

1. **vegetation** : all the plants in a particular place.
2. **preacher** : a minister of religion.
3. **hymns** : church songs.
4. **pipe** : simple musical instrument, played by blowing.

1 **What happened in Chapter 1?**

   a. Why was it difficult for the early colonists to settle in the area along the Hudson River to the Canadian border?

   b. Who were the Anglo-American commanders of Fort Henry and Fort Edward?

   c. What did General Munro ask of General Webb?

   d. Why were Cora and Alice Munro going to Fort Henry?

   e. Where was the preacher going?

   f. Why was Magua important? Did Alice like him?

2 **Who are they?**
Can you remember the numerous characters of the first chapter?
Match the character with the correct description.

1.	General Munro	**a.**	General Munro's oldest daughter
2.	General Webb	**b.**	young Indian guide
3.	Major Heyward	**c.**	General Munro's youngest daughter
4.	Cora Munro	**d.**	a preacher and singing teacher
5.	Magua	**e.**	leader of a small group sent to General Munro
6.	Alice Munro	**f.**	commander of Fort Henry
7.	David Gamut	**g.**	commander of Fort Edward

Past Perfect versus Past Simple

Look at this sentence from Chapter 1:

*It **had been** their home for centuries.*

The **Past Perfect** tense is used when we are already talking about the past and talk about a situation that occurred before that time. Look at this example:

*I knew New York very well. I **had lived** there for eight years.*

3 **Fill in the blanks with the correct verbs (either Past Simple or Past Perfect).**

a. The Indians (move) .... quickly across the forest. They (live) .... there for centuries.

b. The frontier scouts (want) .... to go home. They (explore) .... all the Canadian territory for a year.

c. The girls (say) .... they were exhausted because they (walk) .... for twenty miles.

d. Major Heyward (accompany) .... General Munro's two daughters because General Webb (ask) .... him to.

e. The soldiers (be) .... late because they (stop) .... at the lake to rest.

f. We (enjoy) .... a big dinner, after we (travel) .... for many hours.

4 **Listen to the first four paragraphs of Chapter 1, then say they are true (T) or false (F) by giving a tick (✓) in the right box.**

		T	F
a.	Thick, green forests covered the entire region.	☐	☐
b.	There were few lakes and rivers.	☐	☐
c.	Rainy winters and mild summers were the typical climate.	☐	☐
d.	Only the Indians moved quickly and safely in the region.	☐	☐
e.	The French and Indian war started in 1754.	☐	☐
f.	General Webb was the commander of Fort Edward.	☐	☐
g.	General Webb had to accompany General Munro's daughters to Fort Henry.	☐	☐

Now read the text and correct the false ones.

2.
Hawkeye
and the Mohicans

hat afternoon, after having traveled for many miles, Magua stopped and said, "I can't go on. I've lost the way!"

"What do you mean, Magua?" Major Heyward asked, very perplexed.

Magua's cold eyes looked at Major Heyward, but he didn't speak.

"Are we lost? What can we possibly do at this late hour? Who can we ask for help?" Major Heyward said, looking very worried.

Suddenly, he heard a noise in the forest. It was the noise of footsteps. Three men walked out of the dark forest into a small, grassy area. One of them was an American frontier scout called Hawkeye. He wore the typical clothes of the scout: a green hunting shirt, a summer cap of animal skins, buckskin [1] pants and

---

1. **buckskin** : soft yellow leather made from the skin of a deer.

2. Hawkeye and the Mohicans

Indian moccasins. [1] In his belt, he had a hunting knife, a pouch and a powder horn. [2] He carried a long hunting rifle.

The other two men were Mohican Indians, the old chief Chingachgook and his handsome son, Uncas. They were good friends of Hawkeye. The two Mohicans had joined the Anglo-American forces at the start of the French and Indian War in 1754. They wanted to fight their old enemies, the French and the Huron Indians.

The two Mohicans, father and son, were the last survivors of their tribe. The Mohicans had been one of the greatest and strongest tribes of North America. After years of wars, illness and white settlement, thousands of Mohicans died. Chingachgook and Uncas were the last pure-blooded Mohicans!

Major Heyward was glad to see an American frontier scout. He immediately told Hawkeye that they were lost, and that they wanted to go to Fort Henry.

The scout was surprised and said, "It would be easier for you to go to Fort Edward, it's closer."

"What! Closer!" exclaimed Major Heyward. "But we left Fort Edward this morning

1. **moccasins** : simple shoes made of soft leather.
2. **pouch ... powder horn** :

23

with our Indian guide."

"You have an Indian guide who got lost in the forest – how strange!" Hawkeye said, shaking his head. "Indians here know every deer-path and every stream of the forest. What tribe does your guide belong to?"

"He is a Huron," Major Heyward replied.

"Your guide is a Huron! But the Hurons are our enemy. They cannot be trusted."

"Our guide, Magua, was born farther north in Huron country. But later he was adopted ¹ by the Mohawks. He is now a Mohawk and serves in our army as a friend and guide."

"No! He's a Huron by birth. They are a dangerous race. They steal. They kill! You can never trust them. He was probably leading you into a deadly trap, right here in the forest. The Delawares and the Mohicans are the only honest tribes that you can trust. They have been great warriors ² for centuries," said Hawkeye.

"It is getting dark and we need to find our way to Fort Henry. This is dangerous territory. Can you lead us, Hawkeye?" Major Heyward asked.

"Yes, I can lead you to Fort Henry. But first, we must capture your Huron guide, Magua, and make him a prisoner. Listen to my plan. You talk to him, while my friends Chingachgook and Uncas grab ³ him from behind."

Major Heyward walked over to Magua and began talking to him. Magua, however, heard noises behind him and quickly escaped before the Mohicans could capture him.

---

1. **adopted** : taken into someone's family and treated as his/her child.
2. **warriors** : *(here)* Indian soldiers.
3. **grab** : take with a sudden movement.

INTERNET PROJECT

LET'S VISIT THE PLACES WHERE *THE LAST OF THE MOHICANS* WAS FILMED!

▶ Look at the pictures from the film. Then write a brief description of what you see.

▶ Read about the actor/actress and write a short biography.

▶ Collect all this material in a folder.

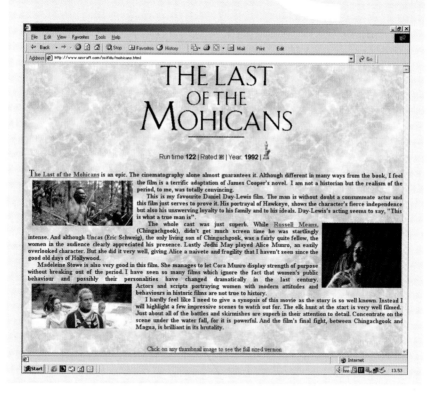

FCE 1 Choose the correct answer (A, B, C, or D). Put a tick (✓) next to the letter.

1. Magua couldn't continue traveling because
   - A. ☐ he was very tired.
   - B. ☐ Alice and Cora were ill.
   - C. ☐ it started raining.
   - D. ☐ he lost the way.

2. Major Heyward heard the noise of
   - A. ☐ footsteps in the forest.
   - B. ☐ other horses nearby.
   - C. ☐ voices in the distance.
   - D. ☐ rifles shooting.

3. Hawkeye was
   - A. ☐ Magua's best friend.
   - B. ☐ Chingachgook's handsome son.
   - C. ☐ an American frontier scout.
   - D. ☐ chief of the Mohican tribe.

4. The last survivors of the Mohican tribe were
   - A. ☐ Chingachgook and Magua.
   - B. ☐ Chingachgook and Uncas.
   - C. ☐ Uncas and Hawkeye.
   - D. ☐ Magua and Hawkeye.

5. Major Heyward asked Hawkeye to take him to
   - A. ☐ Fort Edward.
   - B. ☐ Fort Delaware.
   - C. ☐ Fort Henry.
   - D. ☐ the Hudson River.

6. Hawkeye had a plan to capture Magua and make him a prisoner,

A. ☐ but Magua escaped.

B. ☐ and the plan was successful.

C. ☐ but Major Heyward was against it.

D. ☐ but Alice and Cora helped him escape.

FCE 2 **For questions 1-6 complete the second sentence by using the word given so that it has a similar meaning to the first sentence. Do not change the word given. You must use between <u>two and five words</u>, including the word given. There is an example at the beginning (0).**

0. He usually reads a few pages and then he goes to sleep.

before

He usually reads a few pages ***before going*** to sleep.

1. They arrived home and found the broken window.

after

They found the broken window .... home.

2. The soldiers left the fort and did not speak to the general.

without

The soldiers left the fort .... the general.

3. The soldier found the map because he looked for it in the library.

by

The soldier found the map .... the library.

4. I waited for him for two hours and then I went home alone.

after

I went home alone .... for two hours.

5. The major studied the map and entered the dark forest.

before

The major studied the map .... dark forest.

6. The young Indian ran for three miles and did not stop to rest.

without

The young Indian ran for three miles .... rest.

3.
In the Cave

agua escaped into the forest and was nowhere to be found. It was almost nightfall. At this northern latitude of 42°, the night follows the day very quickly.

Hawkeye and the two Mohicans would accompany the group to Fort Henry early the next morning.

"We must find a place for the night that is safe and well hidden. The trip to Fort Henry is a long one, and there are enemy Indians everywhere," Hawkeye said. "If I remember correctly, there is a secret hiding place nearby. We must move silently, and you must promise to keep this hiding place a secret."

Everyone agreed and Hawkeye led them to the river. They left their horses behind and got into a canoe at the river bank. They went up the river to a small island near a tall waterfall. Behind the

3. In the Cave

noisy waterfall there was a cave, which was their hiding place for the night. There were waterfalls on both sides of the cave.

It was time for the evening meal. Everyone was tired and hungry, but very thankful for a safe resting place. Uncas, the young Mohican, served the meal of venison [1] and water to the two sisters. This attention to the girls was unusual because Mohican warriors never serve women. Uncas sat next to Cora. His eyes smiled at her. He spoke a few words of English, and she was happy to talk to him. They were able to understand each other, and they enjoyed being together.

Major Heyward ate his meal next to Alice. They talked about a lot of things and laughed together. Major Heyward liked Alice and her gentle, innocent ways.

After the small meal David Gamut, the preacher, opened his hymn book and began to play his pipe. Alice and Cora sang some church hymns, while everyone listened sleepily.

1. **venison** : deer meat.

1 **What happened in Chapter 3?**

    a. Where was the secret hiding place?

    b. What did the group eat and drink?

    c. Who served the two sisters?

    d. How did Cora and Uncas spend the evening?

    e. Why did Major Heyward like Alice?

    f. What did the girls do with David Gamut?

2 **Find words in the story that are the opposites of the following:**

    a. daybreak   ....

    b. exposed   ....

    c. friend   ....

    d. noisily   ....

    e. unappreciative   ....

    f. dangerous   ....

    g. disregard   ....

    h. cried   ....

    i. rough   ....

3 **Now complete the following sentences by using some of the opposites from Exercise 2.**

    a. It was almost .... when Magua escaped.

    b. Hawkeye told the group to move ....

    c. The cave was .... by a noisy waterfall.

    d. The group was .... for a .... resting place.

    e. Major Heyward and Alice .... together.

    f. Uncas showed a lot of .... to the girls.

    g. Alice was .... and innocent.

FCE **4** For questions 1-6 complete the second sentence by using the word given so that it has a similar meaning to the first sentence. Do not change the word given. You must use between <u>two and five words</u>, including the word given. There is an example at the beginning (0).

0. If I remember correctly there is a cave in the forest.
   wrong
   If I'm *not wrong* there is a cave in the forest.

1. Magua escaped and was nowhere to be found.
   no one
   Magua escaped and .... him anywhere.

2. You must promise to keep this hiding place a secret.
   tell
   You must .... this hiding place.

3. "I advise you to think carefully before going down the river in this weather," said Major Heyward.
   better
   "You .... carefully before going down the river in this weather," said Major Heyward.

4. Hawkeye said that Magua was a dangerous enemy.
   accused
   Hawkeye .... a dangerous enemy.

5. "Don't leave the horses by the river, Cora," said Uncas.
   not
   Uncas .... the horses by the river.

6. Chingachgook did not expect to see Uncas talking to Cora.
   surprised
   Chingachgook .... talking to Cora.

7. The French rifle is more expensive than the English one.
   cheaper
   The English rifle .... the French one.

The French and Indian War

The French and Indian War was a conflict between Great Britain and France. The conflict broke out [1] in the territories of the northeast, when most of the American continent was still an unexplored wilderness. In the northeast, the British had established their American colonies. Britain was allied [2] with the colonial Americans, while France was allied with the Indian tribes of the region. Both nations wanted to expand their territories in North America.

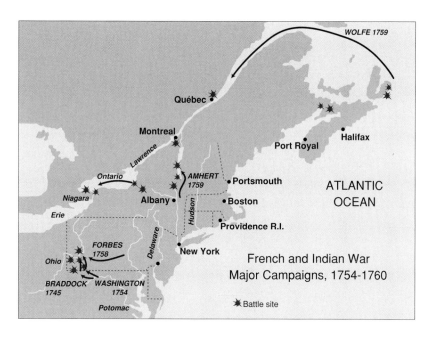

French and Indian War
Major Campaigns, 1754-1760

* Battle site

1. **broke out** : began suddenly.
2. **allied** : when a country is supported or helped by another.

The war began in 1754, when a group of Virginians crossed the Appalachian Mountains in the upper Ohio Valley. They wanted to trade with the Indians and examine 200,000 acres [1] of land that had been given to them by King George of England.

The French were very upset [2] because they thought that the British wanted to occupy their territories. They started building forts to protect their land.

When the news of these developments reached Williamsburg, Virginia, the governor was very worried. He sent a young officer of the Virginia militia to warn [3] the French. This ambitious officer was Major George Washington, who would one day become the first American president!

Washington and a few other soldiers went to Fort Le Boeuf to warn the French. However, they returned to Williamsburg with a polite but firm refusal. [4]

From this point on it was an open war, which took place in the Appalachian Mountains, along the Ohio River and Valley, and along the Hudson River up to the French territories.

The war went on for several years with victories for both the British and the French. In 1759, at Quebec, a very important battle was fought. The British forces were commanded by General James Wolfe, and the French were commanded by General Louis de Montcalm. (The same Montcalm who appears in this story.) In the battle of Quebec, the British were victorious. From this moment on, the French lost their power in North America.

1. **acres** : measures of land (one acre = 4,047 square metres).
2. **upset** : *(here)* angry.
3. **warn** : *(here)* advise the French to stop building defenses.
4. **refusal** : a statement or act that shows you will not do or accept something.

The war ended officially in 1763 with the Peace of Paris. Britain took all of the French territories in North America. France suffered a huge defeat. [1]

The end of French power in North America opened the doors to an entirely new region – between the Appalachian Mountains and the Mississippi River, and from the Gulf of Mexico to Hudson's Bay.

This was a turning point in American history: the opening of another frontier to explore and settle.

The British Attack on Quebec, a contemporary engraving.
Royal Ontario Museum, Toronto.

1. **defeat** : *(here)* when a battle is lost.

1 Tick (✓) the correct answer.

a. The French and Indian War was a conflict between
  ☐ Great Britain and the Indians.
  ☐ France and the Indians.
  ☐ Great Britain and France.

b. France was allied with
  ☐ the colonial Americans.
  ☐ the Indian tribes of the region.
  ☐ no one.

c. The war began in 1754 when a group of Virginians crossed the Appalachian Mountains and
  ☐ wanted to trade with the Indians and examine land.
  ☐ attacked a French fort.
  ☐ occupied French territories.

d. Major Washington went to Fort Le Boeuf to warn the French, but they
  ☐ refused to listen to the warning.
  ☐ attacked the British soldiers.
  ☐ had already left the fort.

e. The Battle of Quebec, in 1759, was very important because
  ☐ the British lost the battle.
  ☐ it ended the war.
  ☐ the British won and France lost its power in North America.

4.
The Huron Attack

Hawkeye and the Mohicans kept watch, while the others slept. Their sleep was interrupted in the middle of the night by the screaming of the horses. There were wolves nearby and they were howling [1] loudly. But suddenly the howling stopped.

Hawkeye was worried and said, "The Huron Indians are in the area. They know where we are. The ladies can rest a little longer, but we must be ready to leave the cave before dawn." [2]

Cora and Alice looked at each other helplessly. Cora said, "If only we had not asked to visit our father at Fort Henry! We have put the lives of these men in danger. I feel responsible."

---

1. **howling** : making loud, mournful cries.
2. **dawn** : early morning when light first appears in the sky.

Major Heyward replied,
"No, Cora. You are not
responsible for this.
We are soldiers and there
is a war. It is our duty to
accompany you safely to
your father."

The Last of the Mohicans

Just before dawn, as the group was getting ready to leave, the Hurons attacked them from the river bank. The screams and shouts of the Hurons were wild and frightening. Major Heyward and the other men fought bravely. David Gamut was wounded.

With the first morning light, Hawkeye saw that four Hurons had swum to the island. He and Uncas shot two of them. The other two reached the island, and Hawkeye and Major Heyward fought hand-to-hand with them. Hawkeye killed one Huron, and Major Heyward had a terrible fight with the other. Heyward was almost thrown off a cliff, but Uncas saved his life.

Major Heyward looked at Uncas with gratitude and respect. Then he said, "Uncas, you have saved my life and I will never forget this. I have a debt [1] with you, my friend."

Uncas offered his hand to Major Heyward. They shook hands and exchanged looks of friendship and understanding.

Hawkeye smiled and said, "Uncas has already saved my life five times!"

1. **debt** : something owed to someone else.

1 **What happened in Chapter 4?**

   a. Why was Hawkeye worried?

   b. How did Cora feel and why?

   c. When did the Hurons attack?

   d. How many Hurons swam to the island?

   e. Who saved Major Heyward's life?

   f. What did Hawkeye say about Uncas?

2 In FCE (Reading), Part 4 you will be asked which person is referred to in the extract.

Look back at Chapter 4 and match the definitions / sentences (1-8) to the correct person or people (A-G).
There is an example at the beginning (0).

A = Wolves

B = David Gamut

C = Hawkeye

D = Cora

E = Major Heyward

F = Uncas

G = Hurons

0. ☐B☐ He was wounded.

1. ☐ He saved Hawkeye's life five times.

2. ☐ She felt responsible for the lives of the soldiers.

3. ☐ They howled loudly at night.

4. ☐ He almost fell off a cliff.

5. ☐ He and the Mohicans kept watch at night.

6. ☐ He and Major Heyward shook hands.

7. ☐ They swam to the island early in the morning.

8. ☐ He had a debt with Uncas.

Each other – one another

Look at this sentence from Chapter 4:

Cora and Alice looked at **each other** helplessly.

Each other and *one* **another** are reciprocal pronouns.
Each other usually refers to two elements, and *one* **another** refers to more than two. (Don't confuse them with reflexive pronouns!)

Look at these examples:
I looked at Alice and Alice looked at me.
*Alice and I looked at **each other**.*

At the ball, the men danced with the women.
*They danced with **one another**.*

3 **Change the following sentences by using *each other* or *one another*.**

   a. Uncas liked Cora and Cora liked Uncas.

      Uncas and Cora ....

   b. The soldiers understood the Indians, and the Indians understood the soldiers.

      The soldiers and the Indians ....

   c. Hawkeye spoke to Major Heyward and Major Heyward spoke to Hawkeye.

      They ....

   d. The Mohicans fought against the Hurons, and the Hurons fought against the Mohicans.

      They ....

   e. General Webb and General Munro are good friends.

      They know ....

   f. The British discussed the problem with the settlers, and the settlers discussed the problem with the British.

      They ....

4 Listen carefully to this conversation between General Munro and Hawkeye. As you listen, fill in the blanks on the map.

Listen again and answer the questions below.

a. What must Hawkeye give Chief Sitting Turtle?
b. Who is David Brown?
c. Who is Major Heyward's cousin?
d. What will Hawkeye find on Rock Island?
e. Who will Hawkeye meet at Arrow Creek?
f. What must Hawkeye bring to Fort Henry?

5. Le Renard

The fighting went on for some time. The war cries of the Hurons filled the air. Hawkeye shot several Hurons with his long hunting rifle. The Indians called his rifle "La Longue Carabine" [1] because it never missed a shot. The army used short rifles, but the scouts were also hunters. Therefore, they used long rifles which were very accurate.

Hawkeye ran out of [2] gun powder, and he asked Uncas to go to the canoe to get some. Uncas went to the canoe, but to his great

---

1. **La Longue Carabine** : (French) the long rifle.
2. **ran out of** : had no more.

5. Le Renard

disappointment, he saw the Hurons pulling the canoe down the river!

They were stranded [1] on that small island, without ammunition and without a canoe. The only possible solution was for Hawkeye and the Mohicans to swim up the river, and get help from General Munro. It was decided that Major Heyward would stay to protect the girls and the wounded preacher, David Gamut.

Hawkeye and Chingachgook jumped into the river and began swimming. But Uncas stood near Cora and looked at her.

"Your friends are already in the river; isn't it time for you to follow?" Cora asked.

"Uncas will stay to protect you," the young Mohican said.

"Oh, no, generous warrior! Go to my father as my confidential [2] messenger. Tell him to trust you. Tell him to free us! This is my wish, Uncas."

The calm, warm look of the young warrior changed to sadness. But he obeyed. With a fast step, he crossed the rocks and jumped into the river. He, Chingachgook and Hawkeye swam away quietly.

1. **stranded** : left in difficulties.
2. **confidential** : secret.

The Last of the Mohicans

They hoped to return to the island to rescue their friends soon. Little did they know of the bad luck that was to follow.

Soon after their departure, the Hurons came onto the island! They began to search everywhere. First, they found the rifles that had been left behind. They immediately recognized Hawkeye's long rifle, and shouted in French, "La Longue Carabine! La Longue Carabine!" Several Hurons stood around the long hunting rifle and looked at it in amazement. They knew that the owner of the rifle was an extraordinary shot. [1]

Major Heyward, David and the girls were hiding silently in the cave. They heard the shouts of the Hurons coming closer. They sat and waited. Cora embraced Alice, who was terrified.

Before long they were discovered by the Hurons. Magua was their triumphant leader! He had betrayed [2] them all.

"'Le Renard' [3] is my French name, and I am truly clever and cunning like a fox," said Magua, his eyes shining with satisfaction. "Now you are all prisoners of 'Le Renard'," he laughed.

He took the girls, Major Heyward and David Gamut prisoners. But he had really wanted to capture Hawkeye and the Mohicans.

Magua and the Huron Indians took their prisoners across the river. Then Magua and five warriors went south with the prisoners. The other Hurons went back to the French army camp.

---

1. **an extraordinary shot** : he could shoot very well.
2. **betrayed** : was disloyal or unfaithful to someone.
3. **Le Renard** : (French) the fox.

1 **What happened in Chapter 5?**

a. Why did the Indians call Hawkeye's rifle "La Longue Carabine"?

b. Who took away the group's canoe?

c. Where did Hawkeye and the Mohicans decide to go?

d. Who remained on the island to protect the girls?

e. What was the first thing the Hurons found on the island?

f. Where did Magua take the prisoners?

FCE **2** **Read the summary of Chapters 1 to 5 and think of the word which best fits each space. Use only one word for each space. There is an example at the beginning (0).**

In July 1757 **0** *during* the French and Indian War, the Anglo-American Fort Henry needed more soldiers. General Webb sent more soldiers to Fort Henry, and asked Major Heyward to **1** .... General Munro's two daughters there. Magua, Major Heyward's Indian guide, led the **2** ....through the forest, but he suddenly **3** .... lost.

Fortunately, the group met Hawkeye, an American **4** ...., with his Mohican friends, Chingachgook and Uncas. Hawkeye didn't **5** .... Magua and said that he was probably leading the group **6** .... a trap. Magua escaped, so Hawkeye and the Mohicans led the group **7** .... the forest.

Hawkeye took them to a secret hiding place to **8** .... the night: a cave on a small island with waterfalls on **9** .... sides. **10** .... dawn the Hurons attacked the group in the secret cave. There was terrible fighting and Major Heyward was **11** .... killed. When Uncas went to the canoe to **12** .... more ammunition, he discovered that the Hurons had taken it away. They were stranded!

Hawkeye and the Mohicans decided to swim up the river to **13** .... help from General Munro, **14** .... Major

Heyward protected the girls and the preacher. After Hawkeye and the Mohicans had left, the Hurons, led by Magua, came 15 .... the island. They captured Major Heyward, the girls and the preacher. Magua was satisfied and said that he was clever 16 .... a fox.

3 **Phrasal Verbs**
a. Look at the phrasal verbs on the left and match them with their meanings.

1. run along		**a.**	find or meet by chance
2. run away with		**b.**	finish one's supply of something
3. run over		**c.**	go away, leave
4. run up against		**d.**	steal and carry off something
5. run across		**e.**	knock down and pass over the top
6. run out of		**f.**	meet difficulties

b. Now put the correct phrasal verbs in the following blanks. Make sure you use the correct tense.

 a. Last night a thief .... the jewels.

 b. "I'm busy now," said the teacher to the children, "please ...."

 c. Yesterday the soldiers at the fort .... ammunition.

 d. The wagon .... a cat early this morning.

 e. After ten years, she .... her old friend.

 f. The settler .... many difficulties on the frontier.

The Origins of the Indian People

The Indian people who inhabited North, Central and South America are believed to have come from Asia, by crossing the Bering Strait, or the Aleutian Islands about 20,000 years ago. At that time, the sea levels around the Bering Strait were lower. A land bridge emerged, making it easier to cross. These people slowly moved from North America to Central and South America.

The first Indians (the Paleo-Indians) were nomads [1] and hunters. They followed herds [2] of big animals, such as oxen, musk, [3] mammoths [4] and antelopes across the continent. When

The Migration of the Paleo-Indians.

drastic weather changes occurred, many animals became extinct in a relatively short time. Much of the grassy grazing land [5] became desert!

A new source of food appeared about the year 9,000 BC. It was called corn, or maize, as Europeans later called it. The Indians began to cultivate corn, beans and squash [6] all over North America.

1. **nomads** : members of a tribe that travels around to find grass for its animals instead of living in one place.
2. **herds** : big groups of animals.
3. **musk** : small, hornless deer.
4. **mammoths** : large hairy elephants.
5. **grazing land** : pastures with grass where animals feed.
6. **beans and squash** :

The cultivation of corn changed the lives of the Indians – they no longer followed herds of animals across the continent. They settled in specific areas and became farmers, although some tribes still hunted large animals like the buffalo.

INTERNET PROJECT

LET'S VISIT A MUSEUM THAT IS DEDICATED TO THE NATIVE AMERICAN INDIAN!
Click on the *Exhibitions* section. Research one particular exhibition which you think was most interesting.

T: GRADE 6

1 Topic – Environment
Choose an Internet text about the conformation of the earth 20,000 years ago.
Think about:

1. How and why the American Indians arrived in what is today called America.
2. How their life changed throughout the centuries. In particular, which animals are now extinct and how cultivation changed the landscape.
3. What we could and/or must do today to preserve our environment.

6. Magua's Revenge

agua led his prisoners through the forest. Late that afternoon, they climbed up a steep [1] hill and made their camp for the night.

Magua went to Cora, put his arm on hers and said, "Listen, you are the daughter of General Munro. You don't know what your father did to me."

Cora looked at him calmly and tried to hide her fear.

1. **steep :**

6. Magua's Revenge

"I was born a chief and a warrior among the Red Hurons of the lakes. For twenty summers and twenty winters, I had never seen a white man. I was happy in my tribe.

"Then the white men from Canada came to the forest and taught me to drink firewater. [1] It made me crazy and bad. My tribe sent me away. I lived alone in the forest until the Mohawks took me with them. I then became a Mohawk warrior.

"The white men have driven [2] the redskins from their hunting grounds. Old General Munro, your father, was the great captain of our war party. Everyone did what he said.

"He made a law that if an Indian drinks firewater, he will be punished. I foolishly opened my mouth and drank firewater. Your father discovered me and had me whipped like a dog in front of everyone! Look at these marks on my back! The spirit of a Huron never forgets."

Cora looked nervously at Magua and asked, "Why are you telling me this?"

"Because I want revenge! [3] I want you to live in my wigwam. [4] I want you to serve me. I want you to be my wife. Then your father will live in torment. [5] This is my revenge. If you become my wife, your sister Alice can return to her father."

---

1. **firewater** : Indian expression for alcoholic drinks.
2. **driven** : forced out.
3. **revenge** : punishment in return for an injury or insult.
4. **wigwam** :
5. **torment** : severe suffering.

The Last of the Mohicans

Cora stepped back in disgust and said, "You want to live with a wife who doesn't love you, and who doesn't belong to your people? It would be smarter to take the rich reward General Munro will give you if you return his two daughters."

"No, the daughter of Munro must get my water, work in my fields and cook my food. Your father's body will sleep among his cannons, but his heart will lie near my knife – THIS IS MY REVENGE!"

Cora was shocked. "I will never be your wife. I would rather die. You are a monster!" she shouted, running away.

Magua was furious. He watched Cora as she ran towards the other prisoners. "Then die!" he screamed, as he threw his tomahawk [1] at the two sisters. It hit a tree above Alice's head. She was petrified. [2] As Major Heyward tried to comfort her, another Huron attacked him. The Indian wanted to kill the major with a knife. At that instant, a shot from a rifle killed the Indian.

Hawkeye and the Mohicans had returned! They attacked the Hurons by surprise. They were able to kill them all, except for Magua, who escaped.

---

1. **tomahawk** : a light axe used by the Indians in war and hunting.
2. **petrified** : very frightened.

FCE 1 Read the text below and decide which answer (A, B, C or D) best fits each space. There is an example at the beginning (0).

Magua and his prisoners **0** ...D..... their camp for the night on a steep
1 .... Magua accused the white men of **2** .... firewater to the
Indians.   Firewater made Magua **3** .... and his tribe sent him to
live alone, until he became a Mohawk **4** .... Magua said General
Munro was **5** .... for many of the problems of his people. The
general made a **6** .... that any Indian who drank firewater would
be **7** .... Magua drank firewater and General Munro **8** .... him
whipped. Magua now wanted revenge. He told Cora that if she
became his wife he would **9** .... Alice go. Cora said she would
10 .... die than be his wife and ran away. In his anger Magua
threw a **11** .... at Cora and Alice, but it did not hit them. **12** ....
Hawkeye and the Mohicans returned and rescued the prisoners.

0. **A** built	**B** created	**C** did	**D** made
1. **A** elevation	**B** mountain	**C** hill	**D** slope
2. **A** bringing	**B** taking	**C** carrying	**D** fetching
3. **A** foolish	**B** crazy	**C** stupid	**D** silly
4. **A** warrior	**B** fighter	**C** soldier	**D** champion
5. **A** dependable	**B** guilty	**C** responsible	**D** answerable
6. **A** commandment	**B** order	**C** regulation	**D** law
7. **A** corrected	**B** punished	**C** beaten	**D** disciplined
8. **A** had	**B** made	**C** did	**D** got
9. **A** permit	**B** allow	**C** leave	**D** let
10. **A** prefer	**B** rather	**C** choose	**D** desire
11. **A** tomahawk	**B** knife	**C** axe	**D** arrow
12. **A** Eventually	**B** Lastly	**C** Meanwhile	**D** Momentarily

Conjunctions

In English we often use words like **when, but, so that, in order to,** to join two sentences and make only one. Look at this example:

It was too dark to travel in the forest. They decided to spend the night in an abandoned hut.

***When** it was too dark to travel in the forest, they decided to spend the night in an abandoned hut.*

2 **Make one sentence out of the two given sentences, by using the words given in brackets.**

    a. It is raining hard. I think we should go out. (but)

      ....

    b. We must cross the bridge. We want to get to the other side.
      (in order to)

      ....

    c. The Indian cut the branch of the tree. He wanted to see the river.
      (so that)

      ....

    d. Alice saw her father. She started crying. (when)

      ....

    e. The men were very tired. They knew they could not stop and
      rest. (but)

      ....

    f. She shut the window. She didn't want the snow to enter.
      (so that)

      ....

7. Fort Henry

The group was again together. Cora embraced her frightened sister, and Uncas helped them both. After a while, they began their trip to Fort Henry. When it was too dark to travel in the forest, they decided to spend the night in an abandoned hut. Chingachgook stood guard while the others slept.

Early the next morning, they continued their trip. To avoid leaving their footprints, they walked barefoot along the stream. Then they climbed a hill, from where they could finally see Fort Henry. What a spectacle they saw! The fort was surrounded by General Montcalm's French and Indian forces. How could they possibly reach the fort?

At this time, Nature became a precious friend. A thick blanket of fog was quickly coming down the lake towards Fort Henry. The fog would hide them as they reached the fort.

7. Fort Henry

Hawkeye led the group carefully through General Montcalm's forces. They were so close to the enemy that they could hear them speaking French and Huron.

Suddenly, they heard a man's voice speaking English. It was General Munro, the girls' father! The fort was next to them. Alice called out, "Father, father! It is I! Alice! Save your daughters!"

He immediately recognized his younger daughter's voice and he ordered his soldiers to open the gates. Tears ran down his pale cheeks as he exclaimed, "For this I thank you, God!"

General Munro was delighted [1] to see his daughters. Cora and Alice were overjoyed to be with their father. He was their only living relative. [2] They had so many things to tell each other. The group was finally able to eat a good meal and to sleep in safety.

However, the military situation at Fort Henry was critical. General Montcalm's forces were much more numerous than General Munro's.

General Munro couldn't understand why General Webb was not helping him. He decided to send Hawkeye to Fort Edward to ask General Webb for help.

Hawkeye returned after a few days and said, "I was able to talk to General Webb, and I explained the desperate situation at our fort. He wrote you an important letter, General, which I carried in my pouch. But on my way here, I was captured by the French and they took the letter. I bring a message from General Montcalm: he wishes to meet you."

General Munro had no choice. He was surrounded by the enemy, he had little food and he had few soldiers to defend the fort. He decided to accept the French general's invitation.

---

1. **delighted** : very happy.　　2. **relative** : (here) member of the family.

1 What happened in Chapter 7?

a. What did the group see from the hill?

b. How did the thick fog help them?

c. Who was speaking English?

d. Where did General Munro send Hawkeye and why?

e. What happened to the letter that General Webb wrote to General Munro?

f. Why did General Munro accept the French general's invitation?

 2 In FCE Paper 2 (Writing) you may have to write a non-transactional letter.

Imagine you are General Munro. You are happy because you have finally seen your daughters, but you are worried about the military situation at Fort Henry. Use the information in the chapter to record the events and your feelings in your journal.

Use between 120-180 words in an appropriate style. You can start like this:

August 8th, 1757 – Many things happened today, both good and bad. Early this morning ....

....

....

....

....

....

....

....

....

....

3 A journalist from the *Frontier Gazette* is interviewing Cora and Alice Munro. As you listen to the interview, complete the table below with the correct information.

	Cora	Alice
Birth place	West Indies	
Height		medium height
Hair Color		
Eye Color		
Birthday	August	
Means of transportation to Fort Henry		
Most surprising thing about Fort Henry		
The thing you like most about living here		_____
The thing you like least about living here	_____	
Future plans		

The Typical American Fort

Forts were built along commonly traveled pioneer routes. They were the only sign of civilization in an immense wilderness. Forts protected travelers and small communities. They provided protection during Indian attacks.

Forts were built and manned [1] by the United States Cavalry. [2] Some forts began as trading posts. Indians often traded animal skins and furs for tools, food and trinkets.

Other forts began as mail stations along the continent's mail routes. A lot of forts became centers of large communities in the West.

Fort Union, a military fort in the Southwest.
Fort Union Trading Post National Historic Site.

1. **manned** : managed.
2. **cavalry** : soldiers fighting on horseback.

Many of today's cities started as military forts. Some of these cities and towns have kept their old names, such as: Fort Worth in Texas, Fort Edward in New York and Fort Laramie in Wyoming.

An engraving of *Fort Laramie* in the 1800s.

INTERNET PROJECT

LET'S VISIT A TYPICAL AMERICAN FORT LIKE FORT LARAMIE! Fort Laramie, Wyoming, was one of American's most important forts because of its location. It was a military fort and it provided protection to settlers who wanted to settle in the West. It was the only place where settlers could find supplies and food products in the wilderness. Find the web site of Fort Laramie and write a brief description of the building.

8. General Munro's Story

eneral Munro called Major Heyward to his office and said, "General Montcalm wants to meet me, and I have decided to accept. Since you speak French, will you come with me to this meeting?"

"It will be a pleasure, General," Major Heyward replied. Then with great hesitation, Heyward said, "General Munro, I have something very important to ask you."

"Speak up, young man!"

"With your permission, I would like to marry your daughter Alice, sir."

8. General Munro's Story

"My daughter, Alice!" exclaimed the General. "You want to unite our two families? But do you know the sad story of our family? You should know it before you make such a decision. Sit down and let me tell you.

"When I was a young man like you, I lived in Scotland. I was poor, although my family was honorable. I loved and wanted to marry Alice Graham, the only child of a wealthy land owner. I couldn't marry her because I was poor.

"Therefore, I joined the army of the King and traveled to the West Indies. There I met a beautiful young girl, who became my wife. She was the daughter of a gentleman of those islands. Her mother, though, was a slave and servant. I didn't care about this. I was proud to marry her. She then became Cora's mother.

"Some people consider these people of the West Indies inferior to us. You certainly know this. When Cora's mother died, I was heartbroken. [1] I returned to Scotland with little Cora. After twenty long years, I again met Alice Graham, my first love. She had waited for me to return! We got married and Alice was born. Unfortunately, she died shortly after Alice's birth. Cora has been like a mother to Alice. Now you know the truth."

"What a touching story!" said Major Heyward, with tears in his eyes.

After a moment of silence, General Munro asked, "Do you still want to mix your family blood with mine? Do you still want to call me father?"

"Nothing in the world can change my love for Alice – nothing. Yes, I wish to marry her!" Heyward answered with determination.

---

1. **heartbroken** : filled with sorrow and grief.

FCE **1** Choose the correct answer (A, B, C, or D). Put a tick (✓) next to the letter.

1. General Munro asked Major Heyward to go with him to the meeting with General Montcalm because
   A. ☐ Major Heyward knew the way.
   B. ☐ Major Heyward spoke French.
   C. ☐ Major Heyward was his close friend.
   D. ☐ he was afraid to go alone.

2. Major Heyward was
   A. ☐ hesitant about going to the meeting.
   B. ☐ very ill and could not go.
   C. ☐ pleased about going to the meeting.
   D. ☐ worried and decided not to go.

3. Major Heyward asked General Munro for
   A. ☐ his permission to marry Alice.
   B. ☐ his permission to return to Fort Edward.
   C. ☐ his opinion on the French general.
   D. ☐ his permission to cancel the meeting with General Montcalm.

4. When General Munro was a young man he lived in
   A. ☐ India.
   B. ☐ America.
   C. ☐ Canada.
   D. ☐ Scotland.

5. His family was
   A. ☐ part of the nobility.
   B. ☐ rich and important.
   C. ☐ poor but honest.
   D. ☐ very well educated.

6. General Munro's first love, Alice Graham, was
   A. ☐ the daughter of a British general.
   B. ☐ a humble servant.
   C. ☐ the oldest daughter of a wealthy doctor.
   D. ☐ the only child of a wealthy land owner.

7. He joined the King's army and went to the West Indies where he met a beautiful girl who became
   A. ☐ his wife and Alice's mother.
   B. ☐ his best friend.
   C. ☐ his wife and Cora's mother.
   D. ☐ his slave and servant.

8. After many years, he returned to Scotland because
   A. ☐ he didn't like the West Indies.
   B. ☐ his mother died.
   C. ☐ Cora's mother died.
   D. ☐ there was a war in the West Indies.

9. He again met his first love, Alice Graham, married her and shortly after
   A. ☐ they went to America.
   B. ☐ little Alice was born.
   C. ☐ they bought a big house in Scotland.
   D. ☐ they went to the West Indies.

10. Cora had always been like a mother to Alice because
    A. ☐ Alice was always ill.
    B. ☐ Alice's mother lived far away.
    C. ☐ Alice's mother died after her birth.
    D. ☐ Alice's mother was very ill.

Modal – will

Look at this sentence from Chapter 8:

*Since you speak French, **will** you come with me to this meeting?*

Will is used to make a request or to promise something to someone.
Shall I/we? is used to ask for instructions or decisions, to offer
services and to make suggestions.

***Shall** we go to the party?*

2 Write the appropriate words in the gaps, using *will, 'll, won't, shall*
in the following conversations.

   a. "The rifles are very heavy. .... you help me to carry
them?"
"Of course, I .... help you!"

   b. ".................... we ask the general for another horse?"
"Yes, I .... go and ask him."

   c. ".................... you read this letter to me now?"
"No, I .... read it now. I .... do it this evening."

   d. ".................... we ask Uncas to guide us in the forest?" asked
Munro.
"Yes, I .... ask him," said the Major.

   e. "Cora .... speak to Magua, because she is very angry with
him."
".................... you speak to him, please?"

   f. ".................... you have a cup of tea with us?"

9. August 9th, 1757

12

General Munro, the major and a few other soldiers were ready to leave the fort to meet General Montcalm. A soldier carrying a peace flag left the fort before them to announce the arrival of General Munro.

General Montcalm was in his tent. There were French soldiers and Indians everywhere. Magua was there too. Montcalm received his Anglo-American guests with respect. He spoke French and Major Heyward translated everything into English. The French general seemed sincere. He told Munro that the Anglo-American position was very weak, and that there was no hope.

He showed Munro the letter that General Webb had written to him.

The Last of the Mohicans

Munro read the letter several times. Webb wrote that he could not help him in any way. He advised Munro to surrender. [1]

Montcalm admired Munro's courage and honesty. He respected Munro's long years of service in the King's army.

He offered Munro and his forces these generous surrender terms: the Anglo-Americans must leave Fort Henry, but they could keep their lives, their flag, their weapons, and their honor as soldiers.

As Munro listened to the terms, his head dropped to his chest. He was immensely disappointed and sad. He and his forces had been defeated. He had no choice. He was responsible for the lives of the people at the fort. After a long silence, he accepted Montcalm's surrender terms. He promised to leave Fort Henry the next morning, and the French general promised not to attack the Anglo-Americans.

A peace treaty [2] was then signed. It was August 9th, 1757, a day of victory for the French, but a day of defeat for the Anglo-Americans.

It was a day of anger for Magua, who did not want peace. That night he spoke to all the other Huron chiefs, saying, "There is no peace for us Indians. The peace is for the white men. We must have our revenge. I want the scalps [3] of the English. I want revenge for what General Munro did to me in front of everyone. A Huron never forgets!"

---

1. **surrender** : stop fighting and agree you are beaten.
2. **treaty** : formal agreement between two or more nations.
3. **scalps** : the skin on the top of the human head.

1 **What happened in Chapter 9?**

   a. Who left the fort first and why?

   b. What did General Montcalm tell General Munro?

   c. What had General Webb written to General Munro?

   d. What were the surrender terms?

   e. Why did General Munro accept the surrender terms?

   f. Who was against the peace treaty?

 2 In FCE Paper 2 (Writing) you may have to write an article.

You are a young journalist for *The Hudson River Gazette.*
Write a newspaper article in 120-180 words about General Munro's
surrender to the French General Montcalm. Use the information in
the chapter and include the following details:

Part 1 – The exact date
                Who accompanied General Munro
                Who was present at General Montcalm's camp

Part 2 – What General Montcalm showed General Munro
                General Montcalm's attitude toward General Munro

Part 3 – Montcalm's surrender terms
                Munro's feelings and final decision
                The reciprocal promises of the two generals

Start like this:

THE HUDSON RIVER GAZETTE

Yesterday, August 9th, 1757, was a very significant day for the Anglo-
American soldiers and their general ....
....
....
....

Now find a suitable headline for your article. ....

Passive versus Active

Look at these sentences:

The soldiers **built** the fort in 1722.	ACTIVE
The fort **was built** in 1722 (by the soldiers).	PASSIVE

We often use the passive when it isn't so important who or what did the action.

3 Change the following sentences into the Past Simple Passive form. Decide whether it's necessary to include who did the action.

a. No one respected the treaty.
   The treaty ....

b. General Montcalm received the Anglo-Americans with respect.
   ....

c. The French general offered generous surrender terms.
   ....

Now change these sentences into the Past Simple active form.

d. Munro's courage and honesty was admired by Montcalm.
   ....

e. The treaty was read carefully by Munro and Heyward.
   ....

f. The battle was won by the French.
   ....

10.
The Massacre[1]

he following morning everyone was ready to abandon Fort Henry. There had been very little time to prepare for this journey. Soldiers, women and children, with their horses, wagons [2] and few belongings, [3] formed a long line at the gate. There was sadness in the faces of the soldiers and the women. The children were frightened and confused. Major Heyward led the group out of the fort.

No one could imagine what was going to happen. The defeated group had just started its long journey home, when a loud Indian war cry was heard. Magua was leading the Huron warriors, who savagely [4] started attacking everyone! The French forces saw what was happening, but they did not try to stop the attack.

1. **massacre** : the killing of a large number of people.
2. **wagons** :
3. **belongings** : possessions.
4. **savagely** : fiercely.

10. The Massacre

Cries of horror filled the air. One Huron grabbed a baby from its mother's arms and threw it against a rock. The baby screamed with pain and died. Then the Huron raised his tomahawk and split [1] the mother's head. This horrible scene was repeated many times. Men, women and children were brutally [2] killed and scalped. Then the Hurons drank their blood. Warriors galloped [3] wildly in circles, killing, scalping and taking the few belongings that were in the wagons. There was mercy for no one. It was a massacre!

Years later, historians called this scene of blood and violence "The Massacre of Fort Henry". Over 1,000 innocent people were massacred here.

Cora, Alice and David Gamut were taken prisoner by Magua, who led them north into French territory.

Three days after the terrible massacre, General Munro, Major Heyward, Hawkeye and the two Mohicans returned to the battleground. It was a shocking scene. Hundreds of scalped bodies of men, women and children lay everywhere. The five men searched the dead bodies. They could not find their friends, but they found a piece of Cora's green scarf and David Gamut's pipe. Uncas discovered Magua's footprints next to those of the girls and David Gamut.

General Munro examined the smaller footprints carefully, and agreed that they belonged to his daughters.

"Let us follow these footprints and we will find the prisoners. This trail [4] leads north. We must go north!" said Major Heyward.

---

1. **split** : *(here)* cut in two parts.
2. **brutally** : cruelly.
3. **galloped** : went rapidly.
4. **trail** : series of marks.

The Last of the Mohicans

They traveled up Lake Horican by canoe. The lake had many small islands, and they traveled close to them for cover. As they passed an island on Lake Horican, they were seen by the Hurons! The Hurons jumped into their war canoes and began following them. Suddenly, another Huron war canoe appeared in front of them.

Hawkeye told Uncas to change direction. Another small island separated them from the Hurons. The Mohicans paddled [1] as fast as they could, and soon they were ahead of the third Huron canoe. The Hurons shot at them with rifles and arrows, but missed them. Hawkeye shot back at the Hurons with his long rifle and killed one of them. At this point the Hurons stopped their canoes and returned to their camp.

The Mohicans and the other men continued their trip up the lake to the northern end. Then, to trick the enemy, they paddled to the east. After a while, they lifted the canoe out of the water and carried it on their shoulders. They left their footprints everywhere to confuse the enemy. At a certain point, they stopped and walked backwards in their footprints. They then put the canoe back on the lake.

At night, they moved to the western shore of the lake, and hid the canoe in the bushes near the shore. They then continued traveling north into the forest. They were now in enemy territory, and their lives were in great danger. Each man was careful not to leave footprints that the enemy could follow. After a few miles, Uncas discovered Magua's footprints again. They were moving in the right direction!

---

1. **paddled** : *(here)* rowed lightly and quickly.

1 What happened in Chapter 10?

a. Why were soldiers, women and children leaving Fort Henry?

b. What did the Hurons do to the group that had just left the fort?

c. Who were taken prisoners by the Hurons?

d. What did Hawkeye and his friends find on the battleground after the massacre?

e. Why did Major Heyward decide to go north?

f. How many Huron canoes were there on Lake Horican?

 2 Read the summary of Chapters 6 to 10 and use the word in capitals at the end of each line to form a word that fits in the space in the same line. There is an example at the beginning (0).

Magua was very **0** *angry* with General Munro and he wanted revenge. — ANGER

He wanted Cora to be his wife, Cora's **1** .... made Magua furious. — REFUSE

2 ...., Hawkeye and the Mohicans rescued the prisoners and they reached Fort Henry. General Munro was **3** .... to see his daughters. However, the situation was **4** .... He sent Hawkeye to Fort Edward to ask for help but Hawkeye was captured by the French who read General Webb's letter. Hawkeye brought Munro an **5** .... from the French general to meet at his camp. That evening General Munro asked Major Heyward, who spoke French **6** ...., to accompany him. — FORTUNATE / DELIGHT / DESPAIR / INVITE / FLUENT

With great **7** .... Major Heyward asked Munro permission to marry Alice. General Munro then told him the **8** .... story of his life. The next day Munro surrendered — HESITATE / DRAMA

to the French and signed the peace treaty. He was
9 .... disappointed.

IMMENSE

When everyone was ready to abandon Fort
Henry, the Huron warriors led by Magua
10 .... massacred the innocent
people.

SAVAGE

Alice, Cora and David Gamut were taken prisoners
by Magua.

Say and tell

We can use both **say** and **tell** as reporting verbs. If we mention
who we're talking to, we usually use **tell + the indirect object**.
We don't put **to** before the indirect object.
If we don't mention who we're talking to, we use **say**. Look at
these sentences:

James **told me** that you were ill.
James **said** that you were ill.

3 Fill in the gaps with *say* or *tell* in the correct form.

a. The women .... that they were tired.

b. The soldiers .... us that they needed new rifles.

c. General Munro .... he was going to the French camp.

d. Magua .... the Hurons that he wanted to attack the
white men.

e. Major Heyward .... the general that he loved Alice.

f. Hawkeye .... that the men must not leave footprints.

11. The French Juggler

ajor Heyward, who led the group, came to a large clearing. [1] In the distance, he thought he saw an Indian village and a strange Indian walking towards him. He called Hawkeye, who looked and then laughed.

"Major, that certainly isn't an Indian village. It's a beaver [2] colony!" [3] he exclaimed. "And look, it's David Gamut – not an Indian!"

"David, what are you doing here? Where are the girls?" Hawkeye asked.

"Magua captured me and the girls during the massacre. Alice

1. **clearing** : small area of land in the forest where there are no trees.

2. **beaver** : an animal, like a large rat.

3. **colony** : group of animals living in the same place.

78

11. The French Juggler

is now a prisoner in a Huron village, two miles from here. Cora was sent to a Delaware village nearby. Since I was always singing my church hymns, [1] the Hurons thought I was mad! The Indian tradition respects mad people, and lets them go and do whatever they want. That is why I am here and free to move about."

"If you are free to move about, then you can really help us, David," said Hawkeye. "You can easily go to the Huron village and tell Alice that we are here to help her and Cora escape. No one will suspect you."

"I'll go with you, David! It will be easier to save Alice if there are two of us," Major Heyward exclaimed. "I have an idea. Chingachgook has lots of paints and he can make me look like a French juggler [2] from Ticonderoga. [3] You know, there are jugglers and clowns [4] who go from village to village. I speak French perfectly, and the paints will change my appearance."

Chingachgook painted Major Heyward's face, and soon he was ready to begin his adventure as a French juggler in the Huron village. Hawkeye and Uncas decided to explore the area around the Indian villages, while Chingachgook and General Munro remained at the beaver colony.

As soon as Major Heyward, disguised as a French juggler, entered the Huron village, he was surrounded by curious children. They looked at him, ran around him and touched him.

Although his disguise was excellent, Heyward was nervous. He

---

1. **hymns** : songs of praise to God that Christians sing together in church.
2. **juggler** : someone who entertains people by throwing several objects into the air at the same time and catching them.
3. **Ticonderoga** : French fort nearby.
4. **clowns** : people in a circus who wear funny clothes and make people laugh.

looked for the biggest wigwam of the village and quietly entered. It was full of Huron Indians, all seated in a circle. Some were talking, others were smoking a long pipe. He sat down with them.

One of the older warriors, probably the chief, spoke to him in French, "Where are you from, white brother?"

"I come from the French fort of Ticonderoga. I am a juggler, a man of magic," Heyward replied in French.

"An evil spirit lives in my daughter. You are a juggler, a man of magic. Can you frighten the evil spirit away with your magic?"

Heyward knew something about the Indian beliefs and superstitions. He thought this was a good opportunity for him to move around the village. Perhaps he could find Alice! He answered the Indian in a mysterious way, "All spirits are different; some can be frightened away, but others are too strong. However, I will try."

"You will try?" asked the older warrior.

Heyward nodded.

"Then let us go to the cave," said the older warrior.

1 What happened in Chapter 11?

    a. Why was David Gamut moving about freely in the beaver colony?

    b. What was Major Heyward's idea?

    c. How did Chingachgook help Major Heyward?

    d. Where did Hawkeye and Uncas go while Chingachgook and General Munro remained at the beaver colony?

    e. What did the "French juggler" find in the big wigwam?

    f. What did the old warrior ask the "French juggler"?

 2 In FCE (Reading), Part 4 you will be asked which person is referred to an extract.

Look back at Chapter 11 and match the definitions / sentences (1-9) to the correct person or people (A-G). There is an example at the beginning (0).

A = Cora   B = Alice

C = Chingachgook   D = David Gamut

E = Major Heyward   F = Older Huron warrior

G = Hawkeye

0. ☐D He was considered mad by the Hurons.

1. ☐ He was disguised as a French juggler.

2. ☐ He painted Major Heyward's face.

3. ☐ He and Uncas wanted to explore the area around the Indian villages.

4. ☐ He always sang church hymns.

5. ☐ She was a prisoner in a Huron village.

6. ☐ He pretended to come from Fort Ticonderoga.

7. ☐ His daughter was bothered by an evil spirit.

8. ☐ He spoke French fluently.

9. ☐ She was sent to a Delaware village.

Before you Read

FCE 1 Listen to Chapter 12 and decide which of the choices (A, B, or C) is
the best answer.
Put a tick (✓) next to the letter.

1. Who was the prisoner of the Huron war party?
   - **A.** ☐ Chingachgook.
   - **B.** ☐ Uncas.
   - **C.** ☐ Hawkeye.

2. Where did the Hurons put the prisoner?
   - **A.** ☐ In a canoe.
   - **B.** ☐ In a cave.
   - **C.** ☐ In a wigwam.

3. Where was the sick woman?
   - **A.** ☐ In a cave.
   - **B.** ☐ In the village.
   - **C.** ☐ In a wigwam.

4. Who had been following Heyward?
   - **A.** ☐ A brown bear.
   - **B.** ☐ An old squaw.
   - **C.** ☐ An evil spirit.

5. What could Heyward do to help the sick woman?
   - **A.** ☐ Nothing.
   - **B.** ☐ Give her herbs to eat.
   - **C.** ☐ Give her some medicine.

12. The Spirit of the Cave

13

Aloud shout came from the nearby forest. The entire village went to see what was happening. A Huron war party had just returned with several scalps and a prisoner. The prisoner was Uncas!

Magua led him into a wigwam, and put warriors all around to guard him. Magua walked proudly through the village because he had finally captured his great enemy. He told the Hurons that Uncas was a Mohican chief and their enemy. They decided to torture and then kill him the following day.

Uncas was tied to a post in the wigwam. He was not afraid of his enemy, who insulted and tormented him. He was a Mohican warrior, the son of a chief. Everyone knew of his courage, strength and honesty. He had always lived like a warrior, and now he would die like one.

The older warrior took the disguised Heyward outside the village, to the cave where the sick woman was. The Indians believed that a cave, with its walls of rock, would protect the woman from the evil spirit that had possessed [1] her.

As they reached the cave, Heyward noticed that a big brown bear had been following him. He didn't worry because he knew that Indians often kept tame [2] bears in their villages.

The sick woman was lying on a bearskin in the dark cave. Lots of Huron women stood around her. Heyward told all the women to leave him alone with her. The squaws [3] left slowly and quietly because they had great respect for "men of magic". Heyward looked carefully at the young woman who gave no signs of life. She was very ill. Unfortunately, she was dying, and Heyward could do nothing to help her.

The big bear had followed Heyward to the cave. It began to growl [4] and to move around. Heyward didn't know what to do with the bear.

Suddenly, the bear started laughing. It took its head off and it was Hawkeye!

1. **possessed** : controlled.
2. **tame** : not wild, not afraid of humans.
3. **squaws** : Indian word for women or wives.
4. **growl** : make a deep sound of anger, grumble.

1 **What happened in Chapter 12?**

    a. What did the Huron war party bring to the village?

    b. Where was Uncas put?

    c. When would the Hurons torture and kill him?

    d. Why did the Hurons keep the sick woman in the cave?

    e. What did the disguised Heyward say to the squaws inside the cave?

    f. Who was disguised as a bear?

FCE **2** **For questions 1-4 using the word given complete the second sentence so that it has a similar meaning to the first sentence. Do not change the word given. You must use <u>between two and five words</u>, including the word given. There is an example at the beginning (0).**

    0. Heyward did not succeed in helping the sick woman.
    able
    Heyward was **not able to help** the sick woman.

    1. The orders had to be obeyed immediately.
    necessary
    It was .... the orders immediately.

    2. Hawkeye remembered to bring everything except his hat.
    forgot
    The only thing .... his hat.

    3. Alice regretted coming to Fort Henry.
    wished
    Alice .... to Fort Henry.

    4. Major Heyward was going to present a juggling show to the Hurons.
    be
    A juggling show .... by Major Heyward to the Hurons.

Present Perfect and Present Perfect Continuous

We use the **Present Perfect** when we are concerned with the present effects of something which happened at an indefinite time in the past.

E.g. *I've forgotten the map!*

We use the **Present Perfect Continuous** to emphasize the fact that a recent event continued to happen for some time.

E.g. *They have been working all day.*

3 Here is an interview with Hawkeye. Create sentences with the words that are given and add words of your own. Make sure you put the verbs into the correct tense.

Interviewer: How long / be / frontier scout?

Hawkeye: I / be / scout / 30 years.

Interviewer: How long / live / forest?

Hawkeye: I / live / forest / 15 years.

Interviewer: Where / be / from?

Hawkeye: I / be / born / Boston / but / I / live / in / wilderness / since / I / can remember.

Interviewer: What / do / frontier scout / do?

Hawkeye: He / guide / people / in wilderness / and / he / hunt / wild animals. He / also / help / soldiers.

Interviewer: How long / travel / today?

Hawkeye: I / leave / Fort Henry / sunrise / and I / travel / eight hours. I / tired and hungry!

4 **Listen to this interview with Chief Chingachgook, and then fill in the blank spaces.**

A journalist from the "Frontier Gazette" is interviewing Chief Chingachgook.

Interviewer: How old are you, Chief Chingachgook?

Chingachgook: I have seen 63 .... and 63 ....

Interviewer: Who are your people?

Chingachgook: My .... are the Mohicans, the people of the turtle. We were numerous and strong before the pale faces came.

Interviewer: What .... when the white men came?

Chingachgook: The .... started cutting the trees in our ...., making .... and .... The .... of the forest ran away. Our people had to move away, ... farther .... The palefaces took our .... and our hunting ...., and gave us nothing.

Interviewer: Did the white settlers bring you anything?

Chingachgook: The settlers brought us ...., death, ... and firewater. These things .... our people, who were once strong and .... Firewater made our men ....

Interviewer: How do you see the ....?

Chingachgook: There is .... and .... in the future of the white settlers, but there is only .... in the future of the Indians.

Interviewer: Why do you say this?

Chingachgook: My .... have seen .... things. In the .... of my life, when I was a .... warrior, my people .... this land. They were ...., strong and healthy. We lived in .... with nature. Now, in the winter of my ...., the white men rule my .... My people have .... This .... world is no longer ....

The Iroquois
Confederacy [1]

Long before the first white settlers came to the area of western New York, there was an ancient confederacy among the Indian tribes of the area. It was known as "The Iroquois Confederacy" or "League" and consisted of the Mohawks, Oneidas, Senecas, Cayugas and Onondagas. These were the tribes of the Iroquois people. Later on, a sixth tribe joined the confederacy – the tribe of the Tuscaroras, that had migrated from the south-east.

The Iroquois Constitution, [2] which was probably created in the 15th

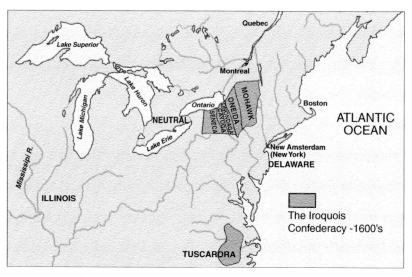

A map of the Iroquois Confederacy in the 1600s.

1. **confederacy** : people or groups united for a common purpose.
2. **constitution** : the system of laws according to which a country or an organization is governed.

or 16th century, has become a model for representative governments or democracies. The confederacy was ruled by 50 male peace chiefs, who were chosen by the Iroquois women. They met once a year in autumn.

The confederacy formed one strong group of Indians who traded together, hunted together and often fought together in wars against other tribes. Their main objective, [1] however, was peace.

The French and Indian War destroyed the unity of this great confederacy. As time went on, the tribes disappeared.

Today nothing remains of these extraordinary people in those regions where they lived for centuries.

The only reminders [2] we have of their existence are their names: today, in New York State, there are counties [3] named Oneida, Seneca, Cayuga, Onondaga. The second river of New York State is named the Mohawk.

The Iroquois Confederacy will remain in history as one of the first forms of democratic government in the New World.

An Iroquis warrior, engraving of the 1800s.

1. **objective** : aim or purpose.
2. **reminders** : things that make you remember something else.
3. **counties** : large areas of a state that have been divided from others for purposes of local government.

1 Can you find the six hidden tribes that formed the Iroquois Confederacy? Circle them.

A	P	X	U	W	S	B	I	Z	C	H	F
O	S	R	C	A	Y	U	G	A	P	E	O
T	M	E	N	J	O	N	E	I	D	A	B
U	K	Q	N	P	A	J	K	W	O	L	N
S	C	M	G	E	O	V	M	K	N	J	R
C	E	O	X	P	C	F	B	D	O	Q	O
A	U	H	W	C	K	A	X	N	N	C	T
R	F	A	B	H	E	T	A	Q	D	G	A
O	G	W	S	D	A	E	D	R	A	M	C
R	Q	K	U	F	W	O	I	H	G	B	D
A	O	U	T	L	G	W	Q	X	A	P	N

2 Think about:
What forms of government do you know?
What are their advantages and disadvantages?

....

....

....

....

....

....

....

....

13. Alice Escapes

eyward couldn't believe his eyes. "Hawkeye, what are you doing here dressed as a bear?" Hawkeye replied smiling, "When I was in the forest, I saw a Huron medicine man dressing up as a bear. I killed the medicine man and took his place as a bear. This is the perfect disguise. Do you know that I found Alice?"

"You did? Where is she?" Heyward cried.

"She's in the next cave. She is tied to a post."

Heyward immediately ran to the next cave and untied her. She was trembling and could barely stand up.

"My dearest Alice!" Heyward cried, embracing her.

"Duncan, I knew that you would never desert [1] me!" Alice

1. **desert** : leave at a difficult time or in a cruel way.

exclaimed, her voice trembling.

"We must get out of here now," said Heyward. But just as he took Alice's hand, Magua surprised them from behind. He laughed in his evil [1] way. But before he could finish laughing, the "bear" grabbed Magua and threw him to the ground. He began to tie him with long strings of buckskin. First, he tied his arms behind his back. Then he tied his legs together tightly. At last, he gagged [2] Magua's mouth. He left him on the ground in the cave. Magua was powerless!

1. **evil** : wicked, bad, immoral.
2. **gagged** : tied a piece of cloth around his mouth to stop him from shouting.

13. Alice Escapes

Hawkeye then turned to Alice and Heyward, "Alice, if you want to escape from here, put on the clothes of the sick woman, and keep your face covered. Duncan, you carry her in your arms. Tell the Indians outside that you are taking the woman to the forest to eat special herbs. Let's go now!"

Heyward, with Alice in his arms, and the "bear" walked out of the cave and they found a crowd of Indians. The father and the husband of the sick woman asked Heyward where he was taking her.

"I have driven away the evil spirit. It is now shut in the cave. No one must enter the cave until sunrise. I am taking the woman to the forest to eat special herbs that will make her strong. She will return to her wigwam at sunrise."

The father and the husband were satisfied with Heyward's explanation, and let them go into the forest.

As soon as they had entered the forest, Hawkeye said, "At this point, my friends, I must leave you. Uncas is still a prisoner of the Hurons and I cannot leave him here alone. We have lived together and fought together for many years. I want to try to save him."

"Thank you for your precious help, Hawkeye," said Heyward smiling.

"There is very little time, Heyward. Take Alice along the northern bank [1] until you come to a waterfall. Then climb the hill on your right and you will see the village of the Delaware Indians. There you will both be safe. The Delawares are related [2] to the Mohicans, and they will help you."

Heyward and Alice began their journey through the forest, while Hawkeye, still dressed as a bear, returned to the Huron village.

---

1. **bank** : *(here)* side of a river.
2. **related** : *(here)* connected by family ties.

1 **What happened in Chapter 13?**

   a. How did Hawkeye find the bear disguise?

   b. Where did Heyward find Alice?

   c. What did the "bear" do to Magua?

   d. What did Hawkeye advise Alice to do?

   e. Who did Alice and Heyward meet outside the cave, and what did Heyward tell them?

   f. Where did Hawkeye tell Heyward to take Alice and why?

 2 **Read the summary of Chapters 11 to 13. Some of the lines are correct and some have a word which should not be there. If a line is correct, put a tick (✓) by the number. If a line has a word which should not be there, write the word at the end of the line. There is an example at the beginning (0).**

Major Heyward and his group find David Gamut who	0 ...✓......
tells to them that Cora and Alice are prisoners in two of	1 ....
different Indian villages. Heyward disguises himself	2 ....
such as a French juggler and goes to the Huron village.	3 ....
A Huron Indian asks from him to frighten away an evil	4 ....
spirit that is disturbing his daughter. Magua finally	5 ....
captures his enemy Uncas and plans to kill him the next	6 ....
day, but Uncas is not be afraid. Inside the cave Heyward	7 ....
sees the sick woman but he cannot to help her.	8 ....
Suddenly, Heyward discovers that the big bear in the	9 ....
cave is Hawkeye. Together they go to rescue Alice who	10 ....
she is in the next cave. Magua surprises them but the	11 ....
"bear" grabs Magua and stops him. Alice puts on the	12 ....
clothes of the sick woman, and she and Heyward are be	13 ....
able to escape to the forest. Hawkeye, still dressed as a	14 ....
bear, returns to the Huron village to rescue of Uncas.	15 ....

Question tags

We add a question tag to a statement when we want to check whether something is true, or to ask for agreement.
A question tag consists of a verb and a pronoun. The verb is always an auxiliary, a modal, or a form of the verb **to be**.
Generally, we use a **negative** question tag after a **positive** sentence:

Positive sentence + Negative Tag

Uncas speaks English, doesn't he?

There was a lot of snow, wasn't there?

... and a **positive** question tag after a **negative** sentence:

Negative sentence + Positive Tag

You haven't got a rifle, have you?

They won't be late, will they?

---

3 Match the statement with the correct question tag.

1. ☐ It's very cold here,
2. ☐ You live in New York,
3. ☐ That book wasn't interesting,
4. ☐ There won't be enough time,
5. ☐ These mountains look very high,
6. ☐ She can't tell us the secret,

a. was it?
b. will there?
c. don't they?
d. don't you?
e. can she?
f. isn't it?

14. Hawkeye Saves Uncas

Uncas was inside a dark wigwam, tied to a pole. Some Huron warriors guarded the entrance to the wigwam. He had been tormented and humiliated by the warriors. At sunrise he would be tortured and killed. The hatred between the two tribes was immense.

Hawkeye, still disguised as a bear, returned to the village. There he met David Gamut and explained the reason for his disguise. David was very surprised, but willing [1] to help.

---

1. **willing** : ready, happy.

14. Hawkeye Saves Uncas

Hawkeye told him about his plan to rescue Uncas. Since David was considered mad by the Hurons, he was free to go where he wanted in the village.

David and the "bear" went to the wigwam where Uncas was kept prisoner. Warriors stood outside guarding the wigwam.

David spoke to one of the warriors who understood a little English. He told him that since he was mad, he had certain magic powers that could make Uncas as weak and cowardly [1] as a Delaware squaw. Becoming weak and cowardly was the worst humiliation [2] for any Indian warrior. It was far better to die a terrible death. The warrior told the others about David's magic powers and about his cruel idea. They were amused and agreed that this spell would destroy Uncas' reputation. David entered the wigwam and the "bear" followed. The "bear" immediately went to Uncas and identified himself. Uncas was glad to see his faithful friend, Hawkeye. While Hawkeye freed Uncas, he quickly explained his escape plan. He took off his bearskin and gave it to Uncas. Uncas was now the "bear".

David, instead, gave Hawkeye his clothes, hat, glasses and prayer book. Hawkeye was now disguised as the preacher. David agreed to take Uncas' place and be the prisoner for a short time, until the Hurons discovered the truth. The Hurons would never hurt a mad person, so David was safe.

Hawkeye and Uncas were on their way to the Delaware village, where they would find their friends.

---

1. **cowardly** : fearful, opposite of courageous.
2. **humiliation** : disgrace.

1 What happened in Chapter 14?

a. Why did the Huron warriors torment and humiliate Uncas?

b. What did David Gamut tell the warrior who was guarding the wigwam?

c. What was the worst humiliation for an Indian warrior?

d. Why did the warriors let David and the "bear" enter the wigwam?

e. When they left the cave who was disguised as the bear and who was disguised as the preacher?

f. Who took Uncas' place in the wigwam?

2 In the chapter you have just read, there are many words with negative meanings – words that describe bad actions or unhappy thoughts.

Look at the words below. Then decide if the word is a noun, a verb or an adjective, and put it in the correct column.

> cruel   destroy   humiliated   weak   tormented
> hatred   cowardly   tortured   terrible   mad   hurt
> death   killed   dark   humiliation   die

NOUNS	VERBS	ADJECTIVES
....	....	....
....	....	....
....	....	....
....	....	....
....	....	....

Now use the words to fill in these sentences.

a. The Hurons hoped the spell would .... Uncas' reputation.

b. Uncas had been .... and .... by the warriors.

c. The Hurons thought David Gamut was ....

d. Delaware squaws were considered .... and ....

e. The .... between the tribes was immense.

f. At sunrise, Uncas would be .... and ....

Phrasal verbs

In Chapter 14 we saw this sentence:

*He **took off** his bearskin and gave it to Uncas.*

Took off is a phrasal verb. A phrasal verb is a combination of a verb and an adverb or preposition. Generally the usual meaning of the verb is changed.
Look at this example and discover another meaning of **took off** :

*The plane **took off** on time.*

3 **a. Match the phrasal verb with the correct definition.**

1. take in	**a.** separate into pieces
2. take up	**b.** get control of
3. take after	**c.** surprise and confuse someone
4. take aback	**d.** deceive, cheat
5. take over	**e.** begin to spend time doing something
6. take apart	**f.** look or behave like an older relative
7. take off	**g.** remove something or leave.

b. Now fill in the gaps with the correct phrasal verbs.

a. The jeweler .... the old clock.

b. She was .... by the polite behavior of the dangerous criminal.

c. Sarah decided to .... painting as a hobby.

d. He .... his grandfather. He has the same eyes, hair and nose.

e. General Webb .... Fort George last month.

f. We were .... by the high price of the tickets.

4 **Can you do the crossword puzzle with these clues?**

DOWN

1. David Gamut is one.

3. Animal like a large rat.

4. Name of French fort.

7. The sixth tribe to join the Iroquois Confederacy.

ACROSS

2. Indian name for Hawkeye's rifle.

5. Very large animal.

6.

8. Indian tribe, friends of the Mohawks.

9.

10. Hawkeye disguised himself as one.

15.
Magua Declares War

At the Huron village, the real identity of the prisoner in the wigwam had been discovered. The warriors who guarded the wigwam were furious because their prisoner had escaped and they had been tricked. Shouts and cries of revenge filled the air. Fortunately, the Hurons didn't hurt David Gamut. However, he was worried when he realized what was happening in the village.

The father and husband of the sick woman entered the cave to fight off the evil spirit that was shut inside. Instead of the evil spirit, they found her dead body! They understood that they had been tricked and they, too, were furious. A few moments after their sad discovery, other warriors found Magua, still tied and lying in the other cave.

Magua's anger was beyond description. He had lost his prized [1] prisoner, and he had been tricked and humiliated by his enemies. He shrieked [2] like a wounded animal. He desperately wanted revenge!

1. **prized** : valuable.
2. **shrieked** : cried and shouted loudly.

The Last of the Mohicans

Magua called a meeting of all the warriors, elders [1] and chiefs – it was a war council. Magua had always been a good speaker, and a leader of the tribe. He openly declared war on those who had tricked his people.

The war preparations began: runners were sent in all directions, spies were ordered to approach the Delaware village, warriors were told to meet before sunrise. Women and children were told to hide in their wigwams.

The next morning, well before sunrise, Magua wore his deerskin robe, [2] with the design of a fox, his symbol or "totem". The war party was ready to leave. They silently followed Magua in a straight line that today is called "Indian file". As the sun began to rise, they crossed the beaver colony. The warriors saw a few beavers moving about and considered this a good omen. [3] They did not suspect that Chingachgook was hiding in the beaver colony and spying their movements.

It was morning when the Huron warriors arrived in the Delaware village. The morning sun lit up the beautiful summer colors of the forest and the village. The air was fresh, and the sky was a clear blue.

The Hurons and the Delawares were both friends of the French. The Delawares, however, had not taken part in General Montcalm's campaign.

In the past, the Delawares had been close friends with the Mohicans.

---

1. **elders** : older Indians of higher rank.
2. **robe** : (here) similar to a long, light coat, made of buckskin.
3. **omen** : an event believed to bring something good or bad.

1 **What happened in Chapter 15?**

    a. Why were the warriors who guarded the wigwam furious?

    b. Why did the father and husband of the sick woman enter the cave, and what did they find?

    c. What did Magua say to the war council?

    d. What was Magua's robe like?

    e. Who was spying on the Huron war party?

    f. Which Indian tribe had not taken part in General Montcalm's campaign?

Relative clauses

We use relative clauses to say which person or thing we are talking about. Relative clauses are usually introduced by a **relative pronoun** such as **which** or **who**.

WHICH refers to things   WHO refers to people

We can leave out **which** or **who** when they are the **object** of the verb in the relative clause, BUT we cannot leave out **which** or **who** when they are the **subject** of the verb in the relative clause.
Look at these examples:

- **the subject of the verb in the relative clause**
  *The boy **who** lives next door is friendly.*
  *The thing **which** surprised me was the price.*

- **the object of the verb in the relative clause**
  The girl you met yesterday lives next door.
  The man I wanted to see was ill.

2 Look at this dialogue between Alice and Major Heyward. Decide whether *who* or *which* is needed and circle the correct one; if *who* or *which* can be omitted, then circle *omit*.

Alice:	The Indian *(who / which / omit)* I met last night really frightened me.
M. Heyward:	Who did you meet?
Alice:	I met the old Indian *(who / which / omit)* lives in the cave. He is the one *(who / which / omit)* speaks French.
M. Heyward:	Yes, I know him. He's a man of magic. The herbs *(who / which / omit)* he prepares are considered magic by his people.
Alice:	Oh, I would never take herbs *(who / which / omit)* a man of magic prepares! I only take medicines *(who / which / omit)* my doctor gives me. My doctor, George White, is a man *(who / which / omit)* studied in England.
M. Heyward:	However, the herbs *(who / which / omit)* the old Indian uses are often helpful. Do you remember the young Indian *(who / which / omit)* broke her arm? The herbal remedies really helped her.
Alice:	Of course I remember her. She is the Indian *(who / which / omit)* served the meal last night.

Before you read

FCE **1** Listen to Chapter 16 and decide which of the choices (A, B, or C) is the best answer. Put a tick (✓) next to the letter.

1. Who welcomed Magua's war party?

   A. ☐ The Huron chief.
   B. ☐ A Delaware warrior.
   C. ☐ The Delaware chief.

2. What did Magua discuss with the chief?

   A. ☐ His recent hunt.
   B. ☐ His war party.
   C. ☐ The massacre of Fort Henry.

3. Who is now a prisoner of the tribe?

   A. ☐ Alice.
   B. ☐ Cora.
   C. ☐ Uncas.

4. Who had the Delawares helped secretly?

   A. ☐ General Munro and Daid Gamut.
   B. ☐ Uncas and Chingachgook.
   C. ☐ Hawkeye, Major Heyward and Alice.

5. What did Magua give the chief?

   A. ☐ A hunting knife.
   B. ☐ Trinkets as gifts.
   C. ☐ A new rifle.

16. The Delaware Chief

Magua's war party was welcomed by the Delaware chief who said, "The wise Huron is welcome. He has come to eat his "succotash" [1] with his brothers of the lakes."

Magua bent his head with respect in front of the Delaware chief. The chief invited Magua to enter his wigwam and share his morning meal. During the meal, the two discussed Magua's recent hunt. The cunning Huron avoided talking about the real reason of his visit.

---

1. **succotash** : an Indian dish of cooked corn and beans.

The Last of the Mohicans

After the meal, the squaws came to remove their gourds. [1] Magua now began to reveal the real reason of his visit.

"How is my prisoner?" he asked, referring to Cora.

"She is well," answered the Delaware chief.

"Does my prisoner give you trouble?" he continued.

"No, she is welcome here," the chief said.

Magua wanted Cora back, but he didn't want to say so.

"Have there been white men in the forest recently?" Magua insisted.

The chief now understood what Magua really wanted. The Delawares had helped Hawkeye, Major Heyward and Alice, but this was a secret. They always protected their guests.

In his heart, the Delaware chief did not like Magua. Magua felt that he was not liked. Therefore, he opened his pouch and gave trinkets as gifts to the chief and his men. These were the same trinkets that had been taken from the dead bodies of the victims at the Massacre of Fort Henry. Magua's cunning move was appreciated by the Delawares. But they still said nothing about the guests they were hiding in their village.

Magua became impatient and said, "I have come to take back my prisoners: Cora Munro and the others you are hiding here."

He had just finished speaking, when a strange, old figure appeared in front of everyone. There was whispering in the crowd.

---

1. **gourds** : containers made from the hard dry skin of a gourd fruit.

FCE 1 **Choose the correct answer (A, B, C or D). Put a tick (✓) next to the letter.**

1. What did the Delaware chief call Magua?
   A. ☐ Wise chief.
   B. ☐ Dear friend.
   C. ☐ Wise brother.
   D. ☐ Wise Huron.

2. Why did the two discuss Magua's recent hunt?
   A. ☐ Because Magua did not want to talk about the real reason of his visit.
   B. ☐ Because Magua liked hunting very much.
   C. ☐ Because the Delaware chief was a great hunter.
   D. ☐ Because Magua was the best hunter of the Huron tribe.

3. Who did Magua want back?
   A. ☐ Alice.
   B. ☐ Cora.
   C. ☐ David Gamut.
   D. ☐ Uncas.

4. How did the Delaware chief feel about Magua?
   A. ☐ He liked him.
   B. ☐ He admired him.
   C. ☐ He did not trust him.
   D. ☐ He did not like him.

5. Why did Magua give trinkets as gifts to the chief and his men?
   A. ☐ Because he was very generous.
   B. ☐ Because he felt he was not liked.
   C. ☐ Because he did not like the trinkets.
   D. ☐ Because it was customary to bring gifts to other tribes.

6. Where did Magua get the trinkets?

A. ☐   He stole them from Cora and Alice.

B. ☐   The trinkets belonged to his family.

C. ☐   He bought them before leaving Fort Edward.

D. ☐   He took them from the bodies of the victims of the massacre.

 2 Listen to the following information about the Indian tribes you have read about in this book. Fill in the table with the correct information. Then, look at the map and see if you can locate the states where the Indians are living today. Listen to the recording more than once if necessary.

Name of the Tribe	Approximate Number of Indians	Where They Live Today
Mohawks	1,500	
Hurons		
Delawares		
Oneidas	4,100	
Onondagas		
Cayugas		
Senecas	850	

T: GRADE 7

3 Topic – Village and city life

Refer to a map of the USA today or use the map on this page.

Think about the following questions:

1. Where, when and why the largest cities were built. When, where and why the urban sprawl took place.

2. Where you would live if you lived in the USA and why.

3. Where the majority of people in your country live today and why.

4. Why you think cities will have stopped growing by the year 2050 in your country.

17. Tanemund

n old figure slowly approached the crowd. He walked with the help of two warriors. His face was dark and wrinkled. [1] His hair was long and white. He wore a long head-dress [2] of colored feathers. His robe was of the finest buckskin. Around his neck he wore big silver and gold medals. These were gifts from white men he had met in the past. The handle of his tomahawk was made of gold.

This was Tanemund, the venerated [3] chief of the tribe, who was sacred to his people. He was the Father of the Delaware Nation. He was over a hundred years old, and very wise and just. [4]

---

1. **wrinkled** : having small lines on the skin of your face.

2. **head-dress** :

3. **venerated** : deeply respected.

4. **just** : *(here)* fair.

17. Tanemund

Tanemund knew about Cora and the other guests in his village. He spoke in a firm voice, "Bring the prisoner and the guests before me."

The prisoner and guests lined up before Tanemund. He looked at them carefully. Then he said, "Magua, you can take Cora Munro because you asked us to take care of her. Now you can have her back. But the others came to our village freely, they are our guests. Guests here are protected."

"But they are our enemies! They are all enemies of your friends, the French, and so they are your enemies, too!" shouted Magua.

Alice, Cora and Major Heyward stood together wondering what would happen to them. Hawkeye and Uncas were in the crowd, trying to decide what to do.

Suddenly, Uncas stepped out of the crowd and went to Tanemund. In front of Tanemund, Uncas took off his shirt so that everyone could see the tattoo [1] of a turtle [2] on his chest. The crowd of Delawares shouted with happiness and surprise, when they saw the tattoo. They, too, were "People of the Turtle". They knew that only the greatest chiefs could wear this tattoo.

"Wise father Tanemund, I am Uncas, son of Chingachgook. I am the last of the Mohicans. I am one of the People of the Turtle. The Mohicans and the Delawares have been true brothers for many years. I ask for your help against the Hurons!"

Tanemund was influenced by Uncas' sincere words. He turned to Magua and said, "Go and take the girl with you, but *only* the

---

 1. **tattoo** : a design on your skin.   2. **turtle** :

girl. The others stay here. When the sun is well above the trees, the Delaware warriors will be after you."

Cora knew the time had come to leave her sister. She looked at Major Heyward with tears in her eyes and said, "I know you love Alice, and I beg of you to protect her always." Major Heyward held Alice's fragile [1] hand, but couldn't speak.

"Alice, let us embrace, perhaps for the last time!" said Cora, her voice trembling. Alice was barely able to stand on her feet, and leaned against Major Heyward. She couldn't believe that she and Cora were separating. The two sisters embraced. Suddenly, Magua pulled Cora by the arm and led her away into the forest.

1. **fragile** : weak.

1 What happened in Chapter 17?

a. How was Tanemund dressed?

b. Why was he sacred to his people?

c. Why did Tanemund say that Magua could take Cora but not the others?

d. What could everyone see when Uncas took off his shirt?

e. What did Uncas ask Tanemund?

f. What did Cora ask Major Heyward to do?

g. How did Alice feel?

 2 In FCE Paper 2 (Writing) you may have to write a non-transactional letter.

Major Heyward has just witnessed a dramatic sequence of events. That evening in his tent he writes a letter to his mother and father telling them about:

a. his adventurous trip from Fort Edward to Fort Henry

b. his friendship with General Munro and the peace treaty

c. his disguise as a French juggler

d. his desire to marry Alice

Use no more than 120-180 words.

Start like this:

Dear Mother and Father,

I haven't written to you for a long time because ....

....

....

....

....

....

....

Countable and uncountable nouns

At the beginning of Chapter 17, we saw this sentence:

His hair was long and white.

Hair is an **uncountable noun**. Uncountable nouns are:
• things we cannot count
• things that have no plural form

Most uncountable nouns are:
substances or materials: air, smoke, water;
feelings or qualities: anger, courage, love;
abstract ideas: freedom, justice, safety.

Countable nouns are people or things we can count. They have both a singular and plural form.

3 Look at these words in the box and put them in the correct column. Some words can be both countable and uncountable.

> paper   umbrella   hair   traffic   advice   egg
> baggage   machinery   news   work   homework   chair
> money   furniture   information   luggage   individual

Countable	Uncountable

The Powwow

Hundreds of years ago, the word "pau-wau" meant medicine man or spiritual leader.

Powwows in the United States today are huge meetings or gatherings of various Indian tribes. They are held all over the nation and Indians from many tribes come from far away. They are usually held at weekends.

A powwow is a family reunion, a cultural revival,[1] an Indian dance contest. But mainly, it is a time for the Indians to find, understand

and appreciate their identity. At powwows Indians learn more about their history, culture and traditions – they learn to be proud of their unique heritage.[2]

There are about 930 big powwows every year, in major cities. A lot of smaller powwows take

A man of the Yakima tribe and a Shoshone-Bannock woman display their costumes at a Fort Hall Powwow.

1. **revival** : becoming strong or popular again.
2. **heritage** : objects, customs or qualities passed down over many years within a social group.

place across the country throughout the year. The main attraction is the Indian dances. Each tribe has its own spectacular costumes and its own rhythmic music. Prizes are given to the best dancer and to the best costume. There are also rodeos and sales of hand-made Indian products.

Powwows have awakened [1] the public opinion to the problems of the Indians. Americans now are much more aware of the Indian situation and its needs. Americans are also learning to enjoy and appreciate Indian culture and traditions. Powwows are an excellent means of communication between the Indians and the rest of America.

1 **How much do you know about powwows now? Tick the correct answer.**

   a. Originally the Indian word "pau-wau" meant

     ☐ strong warrior.

     ☐ spiritual leader.

     ☐ old chief.

   b. Today in the United States a powwow is

     ☐ an Indian song.

     ☐ an Indian tribe.

     ☐ a big meeting of various Indian tribes.

1. **awakened** : made aware.

c. Some of the attractions at powwows are

☐ horse races and canoe races.

☐ Indian dance contests and rodeos.

☐ cooking contests.

d. One important purpose of a powwow is

☐ for Indians to learn more about their culture and to be proud of their heritage.

☐ for Indians from all over America to trade their goods.

☐ to teach the different Indian dialects.

e. Powwows have

☐ many participants.

☐ become famous all over America.

☐ awakened the public opinion to the problems of the Indians.

T: GRADE 7

2 **Topic – National Customs**
Choose an Internet text about American Indian customs or use the dossier about Powwows. Think about:

1. The kind of things American Indians should/shouldn't do at powwows.
2. Which things would be more important for you if you were an American Indian.
3. What people might do to help American Indians preserve their customs.
4. A custom which has been preserved and is celebrated in your country today.

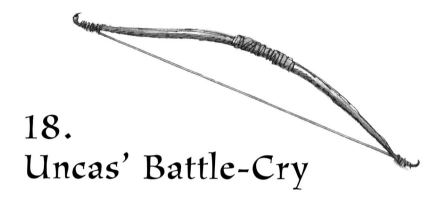

18.
Uncas' Battle-Cry

Uncas, who liked Cora very much, was thinking about how to rescue her. He and other older warriors gathered around a traditional Indian post, painted with dark red stripes. They began to do a war dance and danced around the post. Their faces were painted with war paint. Uncas sang an ancient prayer to the Great Spirit, Manitto, asking for strength and courage. At the end of the prayer, he threw his tomahawk into the post. Then he raised his voice in a fierce [1] shout which was his battle-cry.

The battle-cry was heard all through the Delaware village, and it was the signal of war. More than two hundred young warriors ran to the post. They, too, began dancing the war dance and throwing their tomahawks into the post. War on the Hurons had been declared!

---

1. **fierce** : aggressive, angry.

The Last of the Mohicans

Uncas kept his eyes on the position of the sun which was reaching its high point in the sky. It was time to follow Magua, rescue Cora and attack the Hurons.

The Delawares were divided into two war parties. Uncas led the main party to attack the Huron village. Hawkeye and Major Heyward led 20 warriors to the beaver colony, where Chingachgook and General Munro were waiting. Hawkeye's group would attack from behind to surprise the Hurons.

The two war parties left the Delaware village, and entered the forest that separated them from the Hurons. They moved silently and quickly. The only sound in the forest was the wind.

As they approached the Huron village, Hawkeye heard footsteps coming from the bushes. He immediately pointed his rifle at the bushes, but then he saw David Gamut's friendly face. David was amazed to see an Indian war party approaching. He told Hawkeye that he had just escaped from the Hurons and was seeking [1] help.

"Help?" asked Hawkeye. "We have declared war on the Hurons and we must rescue Cora. *We* need help, David! Come with us!"

David joined the group, and said, "I saw Magua taking Cora into a cave in the mountain. I think he left her there."

"He left her in a cave?" interrupted Major Heyward. "Then we can surely rescue her!"

"I'll take my 20 men and attack from behind the village," said Hawkeye. "Uncas, you and your warriors will attack from the front. In the middle of the confusion, we will go to the cave and rescue Cora."

---

1. **seeking** : looking for.

1 **What happened in Chapter 18?**

   a. Why did Uncas and other older warriors gather around the Indian post?

   b. Who was Manitto?

   c. What was the signal of war?

   d. Why did Uncas watch the position of the sun?

   e. How were the Delaware war parties divided?

   f. Where did Magua take his prisoner, Cora?

2 **Can you identify the characters of the story with these clues? One character's name can be used more than once.**

Tanemund	Alice	Delaware	Magua	Hawkeye
Heyward	Manitto	Cora	Munro	Huron
Uncas	Chingachgook	David Gamut		

   a. Enemy Indian tribe

   b. Great Spirit of the Indians

   c. Le Renard

   d. Mohican who likes Cora

   e. Friendly Indian tribe

   f. Considered mad by Hurons

   g. Young, frightened girl

   h. Old Mohican chief

   i. American frontier scout

   j. Magua's prisoner

   k. Father of the Delaware Nation

   l. Defeated general

   m. Disguised French juggler

   n. Preacher and singing teacher

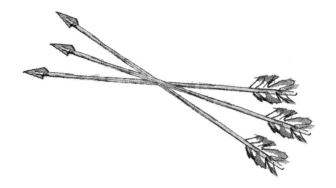

19. The Final Battle

The fighting began in the forest, and spread out to the village. It became a fierce battle. The warriors of both tribes were well prepared for war. There was shooting and hand-to-hand combat. Knives and tomahawks were covered with blood. Arrows flew in every direction. The warriors threw themselves at each other with all the strength and energy of their young bodies.

This was the moment to rescue Cora. Uncas, Hawkeye, Heyward and Gamut climbed to the caves in the mountain. In the distance, Uncas saw Magua with two warriors leading Cora from the cave to the hillside.

"It's Cora, Cora!" exclaimed Uncas, as he and the others moved quickly up the hillside.

The Hurons couldn't move as quickly because Cora was exhausted and could barely walk.

"I will go no farther," cried Cora. "Kill me if you want, you savage! I will go no farther."

The other two warriors raised their tomahawks ready to strike at her. But Magua stopped them. He took his knife and turned to Cora with a look of fierce passion and said, "Woman, choose either the wigwam or the knife of Magua!"

Cora didn't look at him. She dropped down on her knees, raised her eyes and lifted her arms towards the sky. Then she weakly said, "Do with me as you think best."

Magua became very impatient, and repeated, "Woman, choose!"

But Cora did not seem to hear him. Magua, trembling with anger, raised his knife, but then hesitated again. Once more he struggled [1] with himself and lifted his knife to strike Cora.

Just then Uncas appeared, jumping down from a rock above. Magua moved back to avoid him. In that instant, one of Magua's warriors took out his knife and stabbed Cora in the heart! She fell at Magua's feet.

Magua was about to kill his own warrior, but Uncas jumped on him and a long, fiery [2] fight began. Magua wounded Uncas with his knife. Although Uncas was severely wounded, he was

1. **struggled** : fought, argued.
2. **fiery** : angry, fierce.

19. The Final Battle

able to kill Cora's murderer. Then he fell to the ground, looking at Magua straight in the eyes. The Mohican's strength was leaving his body, but his courage was greater than ever. He turned to Magua and looked at him with disgust, as Magua stabbed him in the heart three times. The Mohican was dead! And near him lay Cora.

"Mercy, mercy, Huron!" cried Major Heyward, who had seen the horror.

Magua waved his bloody knife in the air and then leapt [1] across a deep precipice. [2] He hoped to reach the other side of the cliff, where no one could reach him. But his leap was too short. He grabbed a bush on the other side of the precipice. He desperately tried to climb up onto the ledge. [3]

Hawkeye was watching everything from the opposite side of the precipice. He took his rifle "Killdeer", took aim and fired. The bullet hit Magua, who fell to his death in the precipice. Le Renard was dead.

---

1. **leapt** : jumped.
2. **precipice** : a very steep slope on the side of a mountain.
3. **ledge** : a piece of rock on the side of a cliff which is in the shape of a narrow shelf.

1 What happened in Chapter 19?

a. Where was Magua leading Cora?

b. What did Cora say to Magua?

c. What choice did Magua give Cora?

d. Who killed Cora?

e. How was Uncas killed?

f. Where did Magua try to leap and what happened to him?

2 In FCE Paper 2 (Writing) you may have to write an article.

You have just witnessed a fierce battle and the deaths of Cora, Uncas and Magua. You must write a newspaper article in 120-180 words about what you have just seen. Use the information given in the story and include the following details:

Paragraph 1 – Where the battle began
How the warriors fought

Paragraph 2 – Why Uncas, Hawkeye Heyward and David Gamut climbed to the caves
What they saw

Paragraph 3 – What happened between Magua and Cora
The death of Cora and Uncas
Magua's escape and death

Start like this:

THE HUDSON RIVER GAZETTE

Yesterday a fierce Indian war began near the Canadian border, and many people were killed ....
....
....
....

Find a suitable headline for your article. ....

Both, either, neither

In Chapter 19 Magua says:

Woman, choose **either** the wigwam **or** the knife.

We use words like *both, either, neither* **to refer to two people or two things.**

●+●	(?)+(?)	✕ ✕
both	**either (one or the other)**	**neither (not+either)** **not one or the other**

Look at these examples:

Both sisters were afraid.
Please shut **either** the window **or** the door.
Neither the Hurons **nor** the Mohawks liked the white men.

---

3 **Fill in the gaps with the correct words:** *both, either* **or** *neither.*

a. .... Uncas and Magua died.

b. The Hurons will choose to attack .... the fort .... the village.

c. No one was ready for the battle, ... the Indians .... the white men.

d. .... one of the sisters had a rifle.

e. We can take two roads, ... the mountain road .... the valley road.

f. Uncas and his father drank a lot of water. .... of them were thirsty.

20. The Last Mohican

The next morning there was silence and destruction in the Huron village. They had been defeated. The Delawares, who had won the battle, were equally silent and sad. There were no songs of triumph or shouts of success. Everyone in the village mourned Uncas and Cora, the two young friends who had shared a tragic destiny. The entire Delaware village formed a circle around their bodies.

Six Indian girls covered Cora's body with an Indian robe, and sweet herbs and forest flowers. They sang in honor of the dead. Their song said that Cora and Uncas would be together in the

20. The Last Mohican

happy hunting grounds. [1] Cora's beauty had a serene quality. Old General Munro sat at Cora's feet and cried desperately. Alice, Heyward, Hawkeye and David Gamut crowded together in silent grief.

On the opposite side of the area, there was Uncas' body. He was seated, as in life, covered with beautiful ornaments, medals and bracelets. Colorful feathers were placed on his head. Chingachgook sat beside Uncas, looking at the young warrior, and probably remembering their happy times together.

One by one, the Delaware warriors spoke about Uncas; his courage, his strength and his honesty. He had been an example for them.

A signal was given by one of the older chiefs to the girls. Obeying the signal, the girls began to sing, raised the bier [2] and carried it to the grave under some young pine trees. Here Cora was buried in the brown earth.

General Munro stood by Cora's grave and said, "The Being, [3] that we all worship [4] under different names, will remember your kindness, and one day we will all meet around his throne without distinction [5] of color, class or sex."

---

1. **happy hunting grounds** : Indian term for "paradise".
2. **bier** : a frame on which a body is carried.
3. **Being** : supernatural power, God.
4. **worship** : respect and love, pray to.
5. **distinction** : clear difference.

The Last of the Mohicans

David Gamut read several prayers from his prayer book, and then stood silently by Cora's grave.

General Munro and the other whites slowly left the village. Hawkeye remained with the Indians.

Chingachgook stood up and spoke to the tribe saying, "Do not mourn, do not cry. Uncas was a good son. He was courageous. Who can deny it? Uncas has gone to the happy hunting grounds. The Great Spirit needed such a warrior and called him away.

"I am alone now. My race has gone from the shores of the big salt lake [1] and the hills of the Delawares. I am like an old pine tree in a clearing of pale faces. I am alone. I am the last of the Mohicans."

"No, no!" cried Hawkeye. "God has given us different colors, but I am your blood brother. I will never forget your son Uncas. We fought together in many wars, we hunted together in the great forest, and we shared our meals in peace. You are not alone. I will stay with you now, Chingachgook."

Chingachgook and Hawkeye shook hands over the fresh earth that covered Uncas' grave. Tears ran down their cheeks.

Tanemund came to close the ceremony. "My life has been too long. When I was young, the People of the Turtle ruled the world. They were happy and strong. Now the pale faces are the masters of the earth. I have lived to see the last warrior of the wise race of the Mohicans."

1. **big salt lake** : Atlantic Ocean.

1 **What happened in Chapter 20?**

a. What was the Huron village like after the battle and why?

b. What did the six Indian girls do?

c. What did the Delaware warriors say about Uncas?

d. Why did Chingachgook ask the tribe not to cry?

e. Who was Chingachgook's blood brother?

f. Why did Tanemund say that his life had been too long?

 2 **Read the summary below of Chapters 14 to 20 and think of the word which best fits each space. Use only one word in each space. There is an example at the beginning (0).**

Uncas became a prisoner of the Hurons and was **0** ...*tied*....... to a pole in a wigwam. David Gamut, who was considered **1** .... by the Hurons, moved about freely in the village. He convinced the Huron warriors that his magic powers could turn Uncas **2** .... a weak coward. The warriors let him enter the wigwam with Hawkeye, **3** .... was disguised as a bear. Hawkeye took **4** .... his bearskin and gave it to Uncas. David Gamut gave Hawkeye his clothes, glasses, hat and **5** .... book so that he could be disguised as a preacher. David took Uncas' place for a short time. Hawkeye and Uncas were free to go to the Delaware village.

When the real **6** .... of the prisoner in the wigwam was discovered, the Hurons were very angry. **7** .... , they did not hurt David Gamut. When the Hurons found the body of the sick woman and Magua lying in the cave, they were furious and wanted **8** .... They declared war on the people who had **9** .... them. Magua and the other warriors prepared for war and left for the Delaware village. Magua met with the Delaware **10** .... and asked for Cora and the others.

When Tanemund arrived, Uncas explained that he was Mohican, and asked him for help **11** .... the Hurons. Tanemund told Magua to take Cora but to leave the other white guests.

Magua took Cora and led her away **12** .... the forest. Uncas and his warriors prepared for war by **13** .... a war dance. When the sun reached its high point in the sky, Uncas and the Delaware warriors began to follow Magua and attack the Hurons. In the middle of the confusion and fighting, Uncas, Hawkeye, Heyward and Gamut went to **14** .... Cora. Magua, who was leading Cora up the hill, **15** .... to kill her. But since he hesitated, one of his warriors stabbed her. Uncas was able to kill Cora's **16** .... , but Magua then stabbed Uncas in the heart. Magua tried to escape by leaping **17** .... a precipice, but he didn't reach the other side and Hawkeye shot and killed him.

After a touching **18** .... , Cora and Uncas were buried in the Delaware village. Chingachgook and Tanemund realized that "the pale faces are the masters of the earth".

Reported speech

We use reported speech when we want to tell someone what somebody else said. Let's compare:

> **DIRECT SPEECH:** *David said, "I got lost in the forest."*
> **REPORTED SPEECH:** *David said (that) he got lost in the forest.*

When we use reported speech, the main verb of the sentence is usually in the past too. Look at this example:

You met Duncan. Here is what he said to you in direct speech.

"I'm studying French."

Later you tell someone what Duncan said. You use reported speech.

Duncan said that he was studying French.

3 You meet Uncas in the Indian camp. Here are some of the things Uncas says to you:

a. ☐ "I went hunting in the forest this morning."

b. ☐ "David Gamut likes hunting with me."

c. ☐ "I'm teaching David how to hunt with a bow and arrow."

d. ☐ "David learns quickly; just think, he caught two animals today!"

e. ☐ "You can hunt with me tomorrow morning."

f. ☐ "I saw Cora yesterday and she wants to return to New York."

That evening you tell Major Heyward what Uncas said. Use reported speech.

a. Uncas said that ....

b. He ....

c. ....

d. ....

e. ....

f. ....

4 **LOOKING AT PICTURES**
Look at the picture on page 133.

1. Describe Chingachgook.

2. What do you think he is thinking about?

3. Who is standing near him?

Tales and Legends

The story you have just read is said to be true. It makes up the rich collection of American tall tales [1] and folk legends.

For many years after the death of the "white maiden" Cora, and of the young Mohican warrior, Uncas, their story was told again and again. It was told around camp fires, in covered wagons, around the family fireplace and in schools.

Landscape Scene from the Last of the Mohicans (1827) by Thomas Cole.
New York State Historical Association, Cooperstown.

1. **tall tales** : long, complicated stories that are difficult to believe.

After this adventure, Hawkeye continued to work as a frontier scout. He was an important link between the Indians and the white population of the area. He was the first person to tell the story to others.

From Hawkeye we learned that soon after the burial of Cora and Uncas, General Munro's grief [1] was so great that he died.

Major Heyward took Alice Munro to a distant settlement where she was able to smile once again.

It seems that David Gamut returned to teach singing on the East Coast of the United States.

The closing words of the old chiefs Chingachgook and Tanemund were almost a prophecy. [2] The American Indians disappeared from the forests, the prairies, [3] the mountains, and the deserts, and the white men became the "masters".

The Indian Experience

When the French and Indian War ended in 1763, the white settlers began to settle lands west of the Appalachian Mountains. As the white settlers moved westward, more and more Indians were pushed farther and farther west.

In 1763, the Proclamation [4] Line was created. This imaginary line protected Indian hunting grounds between the Appalachian Mountains and the Mississippi River (see Map A). But these protected lands were not the solution to the problem.

---

1. **grief** : great sadness.
2. **prophecy** : a statement about what is going to happen in the future.
3. **prairies** : large areas of flat land covered in grass with few trees.
4. **proclamation** : statement.

MAP A

HUDSON BAY

LAND COMPANY

RUPERT'S HUDSON'S BAY

LABRADOR

NEW FOUNDLAND

NOVA SCOTIA

QUEBEC MAINE

LOUISIANA

NEW HAMPSHIRE
MASSACHUSETTS
NEW YORK
RHODE ISLAND
CONNECTICUT
PENNSYLVANIA
NEW JERSEY
DELAWARE
MARYLAND

INDIAN COUNTRY

Appalachian Mountains

VIRGINIA

NORTH CAROLINA

ATLANTIC OCEAN

SOUTH CAROLINA

GEORGIA

Mississippi River

WEST FLORIDA

EAST FLORIDA

GULF OF MEXICO

BRITISH TERRITORY
SPANISH TERRITORY
FRENCH TERRITORY
····· PROCLAMATION LINE

In 1781, after the American Revolution and the creation of the United States of America, new territories continued to be discovered and explored. The Indian hunting grounds were invaded by the white settlers, all the way to the Mississippi River (see Map A).

Treaties were often signed between the Indians and the settlers to regulate the Indian titles [1] to their lands. However, the treaties were almost useless. The Indians continued to be pushed westward.

The continuous westward expansion was a disaster for the Indian tribes. In 1830, the United States Government passed the Indian Removal Bill. This bill made it legal to send Indians elsewhere. This bill confirmed the right of the settlers to "remove" Indians from their tribal lands. (see Map B)

Some tribes resisted the "invasion" of the white settlers. The Comanches, Creeks, Apaches and Sioux terrorized [2] isolated [3]

1. **titles** : rights to the ownership of property.
2. **terrorized** : filled with fear.
3. **isolated** : apart from other settlements.

settlements, attacking wagon trains and the U.S. Army. There were long wars between the Indians and the whites.

When the first transcontinental [1] railroad was completed in 1869, the West became easy to reach for everyone. The development of the western frontier was very rapid.

Geronimo, Cochise, Chief Joseph and Chief Spotted Tail were great chiefs and warriors. They fought against the white settlers and the U.S. Army for many years, to protect the Indian lands. However, they were not successful.

In 1870, only a very small portion of the United States still belonged to the Indians (see Map B).

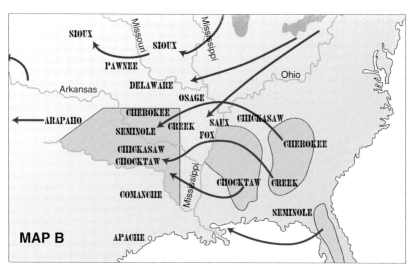

Movement of Indians to Reservations or to the West (1829-1835).

By 1890, the Indians had lost all titles to land. Most of the Indian population had been restricted [2] to reservations on poor lands.

1. **transcontinental** : crossing a continent.
2. **restricted** : limited.

A few Indian tribes still attacked the U.S. Army and the white settlers until the end of the 19th century. Those Indians who survived the wars were placed on reservations, in different parts of the United States.

At this point, the American Indians had been defeated. They had lost their land and their way of life forever.

Sitting Bull, another honest, courageous Indian chief and warrior of the Sioux tribe.

Smithsonian Institution.

INTERNET PROJECT

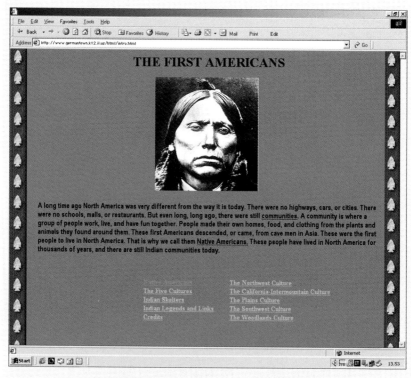

THE FIRST AMERICANS

A long time ago North America was very different from the way it is today. There were no highways, cars, or cities. There were no schools, malls, or restaurants. But even long, long ago, there were still communities. A community is where a group of people work, live, and have fun together. People made their own homes, food, and clothing from the plants and animals they found around them. These first Americans descended, or came, from cave men in Asia. These were the first people to live in North America. That is why we call them Native Americans. These people have lived in North America for thousands of years, and there are still Indian communities today.

Native Americans
The Five Cultures
Indian Shelters
Indian Legends and Links
Credits

The Northwest Culture
The California-Intermountain Culture
The Plains Culture
The Southwest Culture
The Woodlands Culture

LET'S FIND OUT MORE ABOUT THE AMERICAN INDIANS.
Research the following problems:

▶ Native Americans – The Five Cultures
▶ Indian shelters
▶ Northwest Culture – Southwest Culture
▶ California – Intermountain Culture
   Plains Culture – Woodland Culture

Themes for thinking and writing

1 How do you judge the behavior of the "white masters" towards the American Indians?

2 How would you have solved the problem?
Has anything similar ever occurred in your country?

3 Listen to the information about the Iroquois Constitution and answer the questions.

    a. What was the Tree of Great Peace?
       ☐ An Indian god.
       ☐ The symbol of the Five Nations.
       ☐ The house of the chief.

    b. Why is an eagle placed on top of the tree?
       ☐ Because an eagle sees far.
       ☐ Because an eagle is wise.
       ☐ Because an eagle is strong.

    c. Why are thanks given to the animals?
       ☐ Because they give food and clothing.
       ☐ Because they are part of the Tree of Great Peace.
       ☐ Because they represent gods.

    d. Who is the source of health and life?
       ☐ Manitto.
       ☐ The Great Creator.
       ☐ The Great Spirit.

    e. What is another word for "sachem"?
       ☐ Great Spirit.
       ☐ Wise man.
       ☐ Ruler.

f. What must be thrown aside forever?

☐ Self-interest.

☐ Anger.

☐ Criticism.

g. What is the sachem's main responsibility?

☐ Protecting his people.

☐ Thinking about the welfare of his people.

☐ Keeping the peace.

4 The film, *The Last of the Mohicans*, starring Daniel Day-Lewis, was based on the novel you have just read. Certain things in the film are different from the book. What are they? List them in the table below.

Book	Film

Do you prefer the film version or the original novel? Why?

EXIT TEST

Tick (✓) the correct answer (A, B, C or D).

1. Hawkeye and his Mohican friends decided to lead Major
    Heyward's group to Fort Henry because
    A. ☐   the French soldiers were following them.
    B. ☐   the weather was very bad.
    C. ☐   Magua could not be trusted.
    D. ☐   it was very late at night.

2. The cave behind the waterfall was a secret hiding place
    A. ☐   but it was cold and dark.
    B. ☐   and it was warm and comfortable.
    C. ☐   but Alice and Cora were afraid to enter.
    D. ☐   but the Hurons were able to find it.

3. After much fighting in the cave
    A. ☐   Hawkeye killed all the Hurons.
    B. ☐   Magua was wounded and ran away.
    C. ☐   Cora and Uncas escaped by canoe.
    D. ☐   Magua captured Heyward, David Gamut, Alice and Cora.

4. Hawkeye and the Mohicans were finally able to
    A. ☐   take Alice and Cora to see their father.
    B. ☐   take Alice and Cora to Fort Edward.
    C. ☐   meet General Webb.
    D. ☐   take a letter to General Webb.

5. General Munro asked General Webb to help him
    A. ☐   because he was very ill.
    B. ☐   but General Webb refused.
    C. ☐   and General Webb sent him many soldiers.
    D. ☐   because the military situation was critical.

6. Hawkeye was captured by
    A. ☐   the Hurons.
    B. ☐   the French.
    C. ☐   Magua.
    D. ☐   the Mohawks.

7. General Munro accepted General Montcalm's surrender terms because
   A. ☐ all his soldiers had been killed.
   B. ☐ he was afraid to fight.
   C. ☐ he was very ill.
   D. ☐ General Webb advised him to do so.

8. To get revenge, Magua and the Hurons
   A. ☐ attacked Fort Henry at night.
   B. ☐ killed General Munro.
   C. ☐ massacred over 1,000 innocent people from Fort Henry.
   D. ☐ burned Fort Henry.

9. Alice was rescued by Major Heyward who disguised himself as
   A. ☐ a French juggler.
   B. ☐ an Indian warrior.
   C. ☐ a sick Indian woman.
   D. ☐ a brown bear.

10. Uncas was rescued by
    A. ☐ Chingachgook and David Gamut.
    B. ☐ Major Heyward and David Gamut.
    C. ☐ Hawkeye and David Gamut.
    D. ☐ Chingachgook and General Munro.

11. Magua hid Cora in the
    A. ☐ Delaware village.
    B. ☐ Huron village.
    C. ☐ cave.
    D. ☐ beaver colony.

12. During the battle bet   to rescue Cora
    A. ☐ but they could not find her anywhere.
    B. ☐ but she and Uncas were killed.
    C. ☐ but Hawkeye was killed.
    D. ☐ and they were able to escape together.

Score

In FCE (Reading), Part 4 you will be asked which person is referred to an extract.

FCE **2** **Match the definitions / sentences (1-11) to the correct person or people (A-I). There is an example at the beginning (0).**

A = Tanemund

B = Cora

C = Alice

D = General Montcalm

E = General Munro

F = Uncas

G = Chingachgook

H = David Gamut

I = Hawkeye

0. | I | He shot Magua while he was leaping across a precipice.

1. | | He had the tattoo of a turtle on his chest.

2. | | He took Uncas' place for a short time in the Huron tent.

3. | | He prayed to the Great Spirit Manitto, asking for strength and courage.

4. | | He said that his life had been too long.

5. | | His surrender terms were generous.

6. | | His rifle was called "Killdeer".

7. | | The story of his family was very sad.

8. | | Her mother came from the West Indies.

9. | | Major Heyward wanted to marry her.

10. | | He was the last of the Mohicans.

11. | | He had gone to the happy hunting grounds.

Score

3 LETTER WRITING

You have just received this letter from your best friend. Read it and then answer all the questions in the letter.

Dear Jennifer,

Thanks for the lovely postcard from the sea. It looks like a great place and I'm sure you had lots of fun.

I need your advice on something. Before returning to school in September I've got to read a book in English and do a book report. I like adventure stories about American Indians.

Do you have any ideas? Have you read a good book recently? If so, what is it about and why did you like it? I hope to hear from you soon.

Your friend,
Mark

Start your letter like this:

Dear Mark,

Thank you for your letter. I just finished reading THE LAST OF THE MOHICANS... .

The Last of the Mohicans

KEY TO THE ACTIVITIES

Page 14 – exercise 1

Open answer.

Page 15 – exercise 2

1. F   2. D   3. B   4. E   5. A   6. B   7. F
8. D

Page 20 – exercise 1

a. Because it was a huge, unexplored wilderness with many forests, lakes, rivers, waterfalls, cliffs and caves.
b. General Munro was the commander of Fort Henry and General Webb was the commander of Fort Edward.
c. General Munro asked General Webb to send him more soldiers.
d. They were going to Fort Henry to see their father.
e. He was going to Fort Henry.
f. Because he was the only one who knew the secret way through the dangerous forest.
No, Alice did not like him.

Page 20 – exercise 2

1. f.   2. g.   3. e.   4. a.   5. b.   6. c.
7. d.

Page 21 – exercise 3

a. moved / had lived
b. wanted / had explored
c. said / had walked
d. accompanied / had asked
e. were / had stopped
f. enjoyed / had traveled

Page 21 – exercise 4

a. True
b. False – There were many lakes and rivers.
c. False – Snowy winters and hot, humid summers were the typical climate.
d. True
e. True
f. True
g. False – Major Heyward had to accompany General Munro's daughters to Fort Henry.

Page 25 – Internet Project

Suggested web site:
www.ozcraft.com/scifidu/mohicans.html

Page 26 – exercise 1

1. D   2. A   3. C   4. B   5. C   6. A

149

Page 27 – exercise 2

1. after arriving
2. without speaking to
3. by looking for it in
4. after waiting for him
5. before entering the
6. without stopping to

Page 30 – exercise 1

a. It was behind a noisy waterfall.
b. The group ate venison and drank water.
c. Uncas served them.
d. They spoke to each other and enjoyed being together.
e. He liked her because her ways were gentle and innocent.
f. They sang some church hymns.

Page 30 – exercise 2

a. nightfall b. hidden c. enemy
d. silently e. thankful f. safe
g. attention h. laughed i. gentle

Page 30 – exercise 3

a. nightfall b. silently c. hidden
d. thankful / safe e. laughed
f. attention g. gentle

Page 31 – exercise 4

1. no one could find
2. not tell anyone about
3. had better think
4. accused Magua of being
5. told Cora not to leave
6. was surprised to see Uncas
7. is cheaper than

Page 35 – exercise 1

a. Great Britain and France.
b. the Indian tribes of the region.
c. wanted to trade with the Indians and examine land.

d. refused to listen to the warning.
e. the British won and France lost its power in North America.

Page 39 – exercise 1

a. Because he knew the Huron Indians were in the area.
b. She felt responsible for having put the lives of the soldiers in danger.
c. They attacked just before dawn.
d. Four Hurons swam to the island.
e. Uncas saved his life.
f. He said that Uncas had already saved his life five times.

Page 39 – exercise 2

1. F 2. D 3. A 4. E 5. C 6. F
7. G 8. E

Page 40 – exercise 3

a. liked each other.
b. understood one another.
c. spoke to each other.
d. fought against one another.
e. each other.
f. discussed the problem with one another.

Page 41 – exercise 4

b. Chief Sitting Turtle's Camp
c. Blue Hills
d. Beaver Path
e. Tomahawk Stream
f. Silver Lake
g. David Brown
h. Fort Edward
i. Rock Island
j. Pine Point
k. Running Wolf

Tapescript

"Hawkeye, I urgently need you for a very important expedition. You must leave at once and tell no one!"

"I am ready to go, General!"
"When you leave Fort Henry, go east along Beaver Path. Then climb the Blue Hills and proceed East to Chief Sitting Turtle's camp. Here you will give the chief this secret map of the Huron villages in our area. When you have done this, go south following Tomahawk Stream, all the way to Silver Lake. Here you will meet David Brown, the fort's doctor. Please take him south to Fort Edward.
"At Fort Edward, Major Cooper, who is Major Heyward's cousin, will give you a box of new rifles, and a fast horse. Go west to Pine Point. Leave your horse at Pine Point, put the rifles in the canoe and go Southeast to Rock Island.
Here you will find a big box of ammunition, take it!
"With your canoe, go North up the Hudson River, until you reach Arrow Creek.
"Our Indian scout, Running Wolf, will meet you there. Give him the box of rifles, and then proceed North to Fort Henry, with the ammunition. You have 3 days' time!"

a. A secret map of the Huron villages.
b. The fort's doctor.
c. Major Cooper.
d. A big box of ammunition.
e. Running Wolf, the Indian scout.
f. The ammunition.

Page 46 – exercise 1

a. Because his rifle was very long and never missed a shot.
b. The Hurons.
c. They decided to swim up the river and get help from General Munro.
d. Major Heyward remained on the island to protect the girls.

e. The rifles that had been left behind.
f. Across the river.

Page 46 – exercise 2

1 accompany/take **2** group **3** got **4** scout **5** trust **6** into **7** through **8** spend **9** both **10** Before **11** almost/nearly **12** get **13** get **14** while **15** onto **16** like

Page 47 – exercise 3a

1. c. **2.** d. **3.** e. **4.** f. **5.** a. **6.** b.

Page 47 – exercise 3b

a. ran away with **b.** run along **c.** ran out of **d.** ran over **e.** ran across **f.** ran up against

Page 49 – Internet Project

Suggested web site:
www.nmai.si.edu

Page 49 – exercise 1

Open answers.

Page 54 – exercise 1

1. C **2.** A **3.** B **4.** A **5.** C **6.** D
7. B **8.** A **9.** D **10.** B **11.** A **12.** A

Page 55 – exercise 2

a. It is raining hard, but I think we should go out.
b. In order to get to the other side, we must cross the bridge.
c. The Indian cut the branch of the tree so that he could see the river.
d. When Alice saw her father, she started crying.
e. The men were very tired, but they knew they could not stop and rest.
f. She shut the window so that the snow wouldn't enter.

Page 58 – exercise 1

a. They saw Fort Henry surrounded by General Montcalm's French and Indian forces.

b. The thick fog hid them as they reached the fort.

c. General Munro.

d. He sent Hawkeye to Fort Edward to ask General Webb for help.

e. The French took it when they captured Hawkeye.

f. Because he had no choice, since he was surrounded by the enemy, had little food and few soldiers to defend the fort.

Page 58 – exercise 2

Open answer.

Page 59 – exercise 3

	Cora	Alice
Birth place	West Indies	Scotland
Height	tall	medium height
Hair Color	black	blond
Eye Color	brown	blue
Birthday	August	January
Means of transportation to Fort Henry	boat, wagon, horse, canoe	
Most surprising thing about Fort Henry	isolated in the wildness	
The thing you like most about living here	silence and the beauty of the forest	—
The thing you like least about living here	—	afraid of an Indian attack
Future plans	live at the fort and teach children	return to New York

Tapescript

A journalist from the Frontier Gazette *is visiting Fort Henry and interviews Cora and Alice Munro.*

Interviewer: *Where do you girls come from?*

Cora: *We both come from New York, but I was born in the West Indies.*

Alice: *I was born in Scotland.*

Interviewer: *How would you describe yourselves?*

Cora: *Well, I'm tall and I have long black hair and brown eyes. I look like my mother. I'm 23 years old, and my birthday is in August.*

Alice: *I'm of medium height and I have blonde hair and blue eyes. I look like my father. I'm 17 years old, and I was born in January.*

Interviewer: *How was your trip from New York to Fort Henry?*

Cora: *Oh, it was very exciting! We took a boat up the Hudson River for the first part of the trip. Then we rode in a wagon for several miles until we reached Fort Edward. From Fort Edward we each rode a horse, and then a canoe to get to Fort Henry.*

Interviewer: *What surprised you most about Fort Henry?*

Alice: *Well, the fact that it is completely isolated in the wilderness! There are no roads, no people, no other houses nearby.*

Cora: *Yes, I agree!*

Interviewer: *What do you like most about living here?*

Cora: *I like the silence and the beauty of the forest.*

Interviewer: *What do you like least about living here?*

Alice: *I'm always afraid of an Indian attack. There are very few whites and so many Indians!*

Interviewer: What are your future plans?
Cora: I'd like to live at the fort and start teaching the children to read and write. Indian children could attend my school, too.
Alice: I definitely want to return to New York, where I have my friends and my comfortable home.

Page 61 – Internet Project

Suggested web site:
www.nps.gov/fola

Page 64 – exercise 1

1. B 2. C 3. A 4. D 5. C 6. D 7. C
8. C 9. B 10. C

Page 66 – exercise 2

a. Will / 'll
b. Shall / 'll
c. Will / won't / 'll
d. Shall / 'll
e. won't / Will
f. Will

Page 70 – exercise 1

a. General Munro, the major and a few other soldiers.
b. That the Anglo-American position was very weak, and that there was no hope.
c. That he could not help him in any way.
d. The Anglo-Americans had to leave Fort Henry, but they could keep their lives, their flag, their weapons, and their honor as soldiers.
e. Because he was responsible for the lives of the people at the fort.
f. Magua.

Page 70 – exercise 2

Open answer.

Page 71 – exercise 3

a. was respected by no one.
b. The Anglo-Americans were received with respect (by General Montcalm).
c. Generous surrender terms were offered by the French general.
d. Montcalm admired Munro's courage and honesty.
e. Munro and Heyward read the treaty carefully.
f. The French won the battle.

Page 76 – exercise 1

a. Because they had to abandon the fort.
b. They savagely started attacking everyone.
c. Cora, Alice and David Gamut.
d. A piece of Cora's green scarf and David Gamut's pipe.
e. Because the trail of footprints led north.
f. Three.

Page 76 – exercise 2

1 refusal **2** Fortunately **3** delighted
4 desperate **5** invitation **6** fluently
7 hesitation **8** dramatic **9** immensely
10 savagely

Page 77 – exercise 3

a. said **b.** told **c.** said **d.** told
e. told **f.** said

Page 81 – exercise 1

a. Because the Hurons thought he was mad, and mad people were respected and allowed to go and do whatever they wanted.

b. To disguise himself as a French juggler and go to the Huron camp to look for Alice.
c. He painted his face.
d. They went to explore the area around the Indian camps.
e. Many Huron Indians seated in a circle.
f. If he could frighten away an evil spirit with his magic.

Page 81 – exercise 2

1. E   **2.** C   **3.** G   **4.** D   **5.** B   **6.** E
7. F   **8.** E   **9.** A

Page 82 – exercise 1

1. B.   **2.** C.   **3.** A.   **4.** A.   **5.** A.

Page 85 – exercise 1

a. Scalps and a prisoner, Uncas.
b. In a wigwam.
c. The following day.
d. Because the walls of rock of the cave would protect the woman from the evil spirit.
e. He told them to leave him alone with the sick woman.
f. Hawkeye.

Page 85 – exercise 2

1. necessary to obey
2. he/Hawkeye forgot was
3. wished she had not come
4. was going to be presented

Page 86 – exercise 3

Interviewer: How long have you been a frontier scout?
Hawkeye: I've been a scout for 30 years.
Interviewer: How long have you been living in the forest?
Hawkeye: I've been living in the forest for 15 years.

Interviewer: Where are you from?
Hawkeye: I was born in Boston but I have been living in the wilderness ever since I can remember.
Interviewer: What does a frontier scout do?
Hawkeye: He guides people in the wilderness and he hunts wild animals. He also helps soldiers.
Interviewer: How long have you been traveling today?
Hawkeye: I left Fort Henry at sunrise and I have been traveling for eight hours. I'm tired and hungry!

Page 87 – exercise 4

Chingachgook: summers / winters
Chingachgook: people
Interviewer: happened
Chingachgook: palefaces / forests / houses / forts / animals / always / away / land / grounds
Chingachgook: war / sickness / killed / healthy / crazy
Interviewer: future
Chingachgook: sun / light / darkness
Chingachgook: eyes / too many / spring / young / ruled / happy / peace / life / world / disappeared / beautiful / ours

Tapescript

A journalist from the Frontier Gazette *is interviewing Chief Chingachgook.*
Interviewer: *How old are you, Chief Chingachgook?*
Chingachgook: *I have seen 63 summers and 63 winters.*
Interviewer: *Who are your people?*
Chingachgook: *My people are the Mohicans, the people of the turtle. We were numerous and strong before the palefaces came.*
Interviewer: *What happened when the white men came?*

Chingachgook: The palefaces started cutting the trees in our forests, making houses and forts. The animals of the forest ran away. Our people had to move away, always farther away. The palefaces took our land and our hunting grounds, and gave us nothing.
Interviewer: Did the white settlers bring you anything?
Chingachgook: The settlers brought us war, death, sickness and firewater. These things killed our people, who were once strong and healthy. Firewater made our men crazy.
Interviewer: How do you see the future?
Chingachgook: There is sun and light in the future of the white settlers, but there is only darkness in the future of the Indians.
Interviewer: Why do you say this?
Chingachgook: My eyes have seen too many things. In the spring of my life, when I was a young warrior, my people ruled this land. They were happy, strong and healthy. We lived in peace with nature. Now, in the winter of my life, the white men rule my world. My people have disappeared. This beautiful world is no longer ours.

Page 90 – exercise 1

A	P	X	U	W	S	B	I	Z	C	H	F
O	S	R	C	A	Y	U	G	A	P	E	O
T	M	E	N	J	O	N	E	I	D	A	B
U	K	Q	N	P	A	J	K	W	O	L	N
S	C	M	G	E	O	V	M	K	N	J	R
C	E	O	X	P	C	F	B	D	O	Q	O
A	U	H	W	C	K	A	X	N	N	C	T
R	F	A	B	H	E	T	A	Q	D	G	A
O	G	W	S	D	A	E	D	R	A	M	C
R	Q	K	U	F	W	O	I	H	G	B	D
A	O	U	T	L	G	W	Q	X	A	P	N

Page 90 – exercise 2

Open answers.

Page 94 – exercise 1

a. He killed a medicine man who was dressing up as a bear.
b. He found her in a cave tied to a post.
c. The "bear" grabbed Magua and threw him to the ground.
d. He advised her to put on the clothes of the sick woman and keep her face covered.
e. They met a crowd of Indians and the husband and father of the sick woman. Heyward told them that the evil spirit was shut in the cave and that no one must enter the cave until sunrise.
f. He told Heyward to take Alice to the village of the Delaware Indians, where they would both be safe.

Page 94 – exercise 2

1 to **2** ✔ **3** such **4** from **5** ✔ **6** ✔
7 be **8** to **9** ✔ **10** ✔ **11** she **12** ✔
13 be **14** ✔ **15** of

Page 95 – exercise 3

1. f. **2.** d. **3.** a. **4.** b. **5.** c. **6.** e.

Page 98 – exercise 1

a. Because they hated him immensely.
b. He told him that since he was mad he had certain magic powers that could make Uncas as weak and cowardly as a Delaware squaw.
c. Becoming weak and cowardly was the worst humiliation for an Indian warrior.
d. Because they were amused and thought that David's spell would destroy Uncas' reputation.

e. Uncas was disguised as the bear and Hawkeye was disguised as the preacher.

f. David Gamut.

Page 98 – exercise 2

NOUNS: hatred, death, humiliation
VERBS: destroy, humiliated, tormented, tortured, hurt, killed, die
ADJECTIVES: cruel, weak, cowardly, terrible, mad, dark

a. destroy **b.** humiliated / tormented
c. mad **d.** weak / cowardly **e.** hatred
f. tortured / killed

Page 99 – exercise 3a

1. d. **2.** e. **3.** f. **4.** c. **5.** b. **6.** a.
7. g.

Page 100 – exercise 3b

a. took apart
b. taken in
c. take up
d. takes after
e. took over
f. taken aback

Page 100 – exercise 4

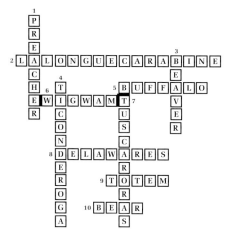

Page 104 – exercise 1

a. Because their prisoner had escaped and they had been tricked.

b. Because they wanted to fight off the evil spirit that was shut inside. They found her dead body.

c. He openly declared war on those who had tricked his people.

d. It was made of deerskin with the design of a fox.

e. Chingachgook.

f. The Delawares.

Page 105 – exercise 2

omit / who / who / omit / omit / omit / who / omit / who / who

Page 106 – exercise 1

1. C. **2.** A. **3.** B. **4.** C. **5.** B.

Page 109 – exercise 1

1. D. **2.** A. **3.** B **4.** D. **5.** B. **6.** D.

Page 110 – exercise 2

Name of the Tribe	Approximate Number of Indians	Where They Live Today
Mohawks	1,500	East end of Lake Ontario
Hurons	1,250	Ohio, Kansas and Ontario, Canada
Delawares	2,000	Oklahoma
Oneidas	4,100	New York, northern Wisconsin
Onondagas	1,400	Onondaga County, New York
Cayugas	550	Oklahoma
	400	New York
Senecas	7,000	New York, Ontario and Pennsylvania
	850	Oklahoma

Tapescript

Listen to the following information about the Indian tribes you have read about in this book. Then fill in the table with the correct information. After, look at the map and see if you can locate the states where the Indians are living today.

In The Last of the Mohicans, *we have read about several Indian tribes: the Mohicans, the Mohawks, the Hurons, the Delawares. What happened to them through the years? And, what happened to the tribes of the Iroquois Confederacy?*

The Mohawks: most of the 1,500 Mohawks today live on the Grand River Reserve, near the east end of Lake Ontario.

The Hurons: today, about 1,250 Hurons live on reservations in Ohio, Kansas and Ontario, Canada.

The Delawares: about 2,000 Delawares live in the state of Oklahoma.

The Oneidas: today 4,100 Oneidas live on the Oneida Reservation in New York, and in northern Wisconsin.

The Onondagas: about 1,400 Onondagas still live in Onondaga County, New York.

The Cayugas: there are about 550 Cayugas in Oklahoma and 400 in New York.

The Senecas: this is the most numerous group, with 7,000 Senecas in New York, Ontario and Pennsylvania and 850 in Oklahoma.

Page 111 – exercise 3

Open answers.

Page 115 – exercise 1

a. He wore a long head-dress of colored feathers and a robe of the finest buckskin. Around his neck he wore silver and gold medals.

b. Because he was over a hundred years old and he was the Father of the Delaware Nation.

c. Because Magua had asked the Delawares to take care of Cora, but the others went to the Delaware village freely.

d. The tattoo of a turtle on his chest.

e. He asked for help against the Hurons.

f. She asked him to protect Alice.

g. She couldn't believe that she and Cora were separating.

Page 115 – exercise 2

Open answer.

Page 116 – exercise 3

Countable: paper, hair, umbrella, egg, chair, individual

Uncountable: paper, hair, traffic, advice, baggage, machinery, news, work, homework, money, furniture, information, luggage

Page 118 – exercise 1

a. spiritual leader.

b. a big meeting of various Indian tribes.

c. Indian dance contests and rodeos.

d. for Indians to learn more about their culture and to be proud of their heritage.

e. awakened the public opinion to the problems of the Indians.

Page 119 – exercise 2

Open answers.

Page 123 – exercise 1

a. They did a war dance and danced around the post.

b. Manitto was the Great Spirit of the Indians.

c. The signal of war consisted in throwing a tomahawk into the post and giving a fierce shout which was the battle-cry.
d. Because when it reached its high point in the sky it was time to follow Magua, rescue Cora and attack the Hurons.
e. They were divided into two parties. Uncas led the main party and Hawkeye and Major Heyward led the other 20 warriors.
f. He took Cora to a cave in the mountain.

Page 123 – exercise 2

a. Huron **b.** Manitto **c.** Magua **d.** Uncas **e.** Delaware **f.** David Gamut **g.** Alice **h.** Chingachgook **i.** Hawkeye **j.** Cora **k.** Tanemund **l.** Munro **m.** Heyward **n.** David Gamut

Page 128 – exercise 1

a. He was leading Cora from the cave to the hillside.
b. She said, "I will go no farther! Kill me if you want, you savage! I will go no farther."
c. She could choose either the wigwam or the knife of Magua.
d. One of Magua's warriors.
e. Magua stabbed him in the heart three times.
f. He tried to leap to the other side of the cliff, but his leap was too short. Then he tried to climb up onto the ledge but Hawkeye saw him, shot him and Magua fell to his death in the precipice.

Page 128 – exercise 2

Open answer.

Page 129 – exercise 3

a. Both **b.** either / or **c.** neither / nor **d.** Neither **e.** either / or **f.** Both

Page 134 – exercise 1

a. There was silence and destruction in the Huron village because they had been defeated.
b. They covered Cora's body with an Indian robe, sweet herbs and forest flowers. Then they sang in honor of the dead.
c. They spoke about his courage, strength and honesty.
d. Because Uncas had been a good, courageous son, and he had gone to the happy hunting grounds.
e. Hawkeye.
f. Because he had lived to see the pale faces become masters of the earth.

Page 134 – exercise 2

1 mad **2** into **3** who **4** off **5** prayer **6** identity **7** However **8** revenge **9** tricked **10** chief **11** against **12** into **13** dancing **14** rescue **15** tried **16** murderer **17** over **18** ceremony

Page 136 – exercise 3

a. Uncas said that he had been hunting in the forest that morning.
b. He said David Gamut liked hunting with him.
c. He said that he was teaching David how to hunt with a bow and arrow.
d. He said David learned quickly and had caught two animals that day!
e. He said that I could hunt with him the following morning.
f. He said he had seen Cora the previous day and she wanted to return to New York.

Page 136 – exercise 4

Open answers.

Page 142 – Internet Project

Suggested web site:
www.germantown.k12.il.us/html/intro.html

Page 143 – exercises 1-2

Open answers.

Page 143 – exercise 3

a. the symbol of the Five Nations.
b. because an eagle sees far.
c. because they give food and clothing.
d. the Great Creator.
e. ruler.
f. self-interest.
g. thinking about the welfare of his people.

Tapescript

The famous "Iroquois Constitution" was probably created during the fifteenth century. This Constitution was the basis for the Iroquois Confederacy, or Iroquois League. The political system of the Iroquois people has been a model for all forms of representative governments, or democracies, including the United States Government.
Here are some parts of the Iroquois Constitution that clearly show the wisdom and justice of these people.
"I am Dekanawidah, and with the Five Nations (the Mohawk, Oneida, Cayuga, Onondaga, Seneca), I plant the Tree of the Great Peace.
We place at the top of the tree an eagle who is able to see far. If he sees any evil approaching or any danger threatening, he will at once warn the people of the Confederacy.
We will offer thanks to the earth where men live, to the streams of water, the springs, and the lakes: thanks to the maize, the fruits, the medicinal herbs and trees; thanks to the forest trees for their usefulness, to the animals that serve as food and give their skins for clothing; thanks to the winds, the rains, the sun, the moon, to all the messengers of the Great Creator, who lives in the Heavens above, who gives all the things useful to men and who is the source and the ruler of health and life.
The 50 "sachems", rulers, or male peace chiefs, will be chosen by the Iroquois women. These sachems will be crowned with the deer's antlers. A sachem must be a mentor of the people of the Confederacy. He must not indulge in anger, offensive actions and criticism. In his heart there will be peace and good. His mind will be filled with welfare for the people of the Confederacy.
Self-interest must be thrown aside forever.
Look and listen for the welfare of the people, and always remember not only the present, but also the future generations: the unborn nation.

Page 144 – exercise 4

Book	Film
Chingachgook is old.	Chingachgook is middle-aged.
Cora loves Uncas.	Cora loves Hawkeye.
Cora is killed.	At the end of the film Cora is alive and Alice kills herself by jumping off a cliff.

1

1. C. 2. D. 3. D. 4. A. 5. D. 6. B. 7. D. 8. C. 9. A. 10. C. 11. A. 12. B.

2

1. F. 2. H. 3. F. 4. A. 5. D. 6. I. 7. E. 8. B. 9. C. 10. G. 11. F.

3

Open answer.